Blood Tipped Roses

Sally Marsh

Copyright © 2021 By Sally Marsh

All rights reserved. No part of this book may be reproduced or used in any manner without written permission of the copyright owner except for the use of quotations in a book review.

This is a work of fiction, names, characters, places and incidents either are a product of the author's imagination or are used fictitiously. Any resemblance to actual persons, living or dead, events or locales is entirely coincidental

First paperback edition September 2021

ISBN 9798456770820

Published Independently
by Amazon KDP

Also, by Sally Marsh

Adult fiction

The Gorse series

Cobwebs on the Gorse
The Agister's Wife

Young adult

High Forest Farm Series
High Forest Farm – Snow Prince
High Forest Farm – Mystery
High Forest Farm – Fly

Non-fiction
Bloody Single

About the author:
Sally Marsh lives in the beautiful New Forest national park, England. A keen writer and photographer, when she is not busy writing she can usually be found wandering across the open moorlands, camera in hand searching for her herd of wild ponies and seeking out inspiration for her next book.
For more information on Sally and her books please visit www.booksbysally.co.uk

This book is dedicated to my incredible husband Chris,
my rock, my soul mate and my best friend.

"Roses can be red, peonies can be pink, and vengeance might be coming sooner than you think."

Vengeance they say is punishment inflicted or retribution exacted for an injury or wrongdoing.

That sounds good to me.

Prologue

On the outside, to everyone that visits my quaint little florist shop, I am what you would call the pinnacle of an English rose. My softly curled, long blonde hair is piled carefully on top of my head in a perfect messy bun and my look is always set on the girl next door image. In my shop I need my customers to see me as someone who they could trust to do their wedding bouquets or funeral flowers, but after I close up for the night, my hair is let down and it's time for my other profession… a much darker one. You see, what I found out a long time ago was that there are people out there, a lot of them, who are willing to pay to get vengeance or revenge, whatever you wish to call it, on someone who has done them wrong, when they are too vulnerable, or too chicken, to do it themselves.

    Have you ever heard of the dark web? It's a place where, if you are desperate enough you can hire someone to do your dirty deeds. Access can only be gained through those in the know and, for the right amount of money, you can hire anyone to do anything, literally! I like to think that I bring a little bit of light to the dark web in some small way.

Are you surprised? Most people are but mostly people are intrigued. Don't tell me you have never been wronged and wished there was some way of clicking your fingers and making it, oh, so right again?

My job can of course be dangerous but that's part of the fun, right? In all seriousness though, I wouldn't be doing what I'm doing if I didn't think that, in some small way, I was contributing to putting the world back on its rightful kilter. I now have a great team by my side and the future is looking bright for our growing business. The pay is wonderful but seeing those who have truly wronged get their comeuppance is worth more than any money, gold or even diamonds. You see, the beauty in our line of work is that you can choose what you get paid and I price up each job depending on how much I like or dislike those hiring me. I also pick and choose what jobs I take, and I always make sure that the vengeance is warranted before I take on any job. I must be careful of course, as the authorities don't really support what I do, although, I think I am actually doing them a very valuable service. In reality, it's only under very special circumstances that anyone actually gets really, really hurt…

I can tell you are shocked, but I can also tell you are now very curious to find out more.

My name is Velvet Darke and I am inviting you into my world. Are you ready?

***

The officer is starting to look a bit fractious and small beads of sweat are beginning to form across his brow. He is flicking through a cardboard bound file of papers repeatedly, each time a little faster than the last, like a build-up of speed is going to help him find what he is looking for. With a sigh and a quick clear of his throat he admits defeat and drops the file onto the well-worn wooden table that I am sitting behind.

"Am I free to go now?" I ask, while applying a fresh layer of shiny lip gloss to my already shiny lips.

"Just answer me one thing Miss Darke. Why do you not see that what you do for a living is a problem?" He asks bluntly, now fiddling with the button on the cuff of his right shirt sleeve.

"Have I done anything illegal, officer?" I reply with a sweet smile, my head tilted slightly.

"You walk a very tight line and you know it," he grunts, slipping on the dark suit jacket that had been hung on the back of his chair.

"We both have a different opinion on that so let's agree to disagree, shall we?" I sigh, getting to my feet and stretching, almost cat-like, as the numbness from sitting on a hard plastic chair eases away. "Perhaps Sir, you need to consider that maybe I'm not part of the problem I'm actually part of the solution?"

The officer doesn't reply. He just opens the interview door wide and glares as I head past him and down the corridor, the sound of my high heels echoing behind me.

Chapter One

I have always loved flowers, even as a child. My mother kept our garden at my childhood home in England filled to the brim with every type of plant and flower. Some of the best days of my childhood were spent playing amongst them. When I was fourteen she suddenly announced we were moving to Los Angeles to live with some 'cousins' of hers and within a week we were gone, leaving our home and beautiful garden behind. I had been an awkward, gawky child who never seemed to make solid friends, so leaving hadn't been particularly heart-breaking, except leaving the garden behind along with all its memories.

    I opened my own small florist shop, which I named 'Lily's', after my mother, in my hometown of Brinton, Los Angeles three years ago, when I was 24 and I have grown the business from there. I work hard, I always have, and if I set my mind to something I can promise you I will achieve it. I'm a bit of a perfectionist and I like things to be just right. That goes for everything that I do, from the way I dress to the way I work; I like things just so.

"Velvet Darke: Revenge Artist", was not something I planned, more kind of happened on impulse.

***

It all started one day in March when I was delivering a huge bouquet of Mother's Day roses to a beautiful red bricked house a couple of minutes away from the shop. I had made the delivery, exchanged the usual pleasantries with the delighted recipient and was returning to my van when I caught the sound of crying coming over the high wooden fence next door. It was the sort of crying that stops you in your tracks and begs you to follow it, so after a brief hesitation that is exactly what I did.

I recall clearly how I tiptoed up the gravel drive, following the unrelenting sobs, until I could see a woman, sitting on her back porch doorstep, head in hands, crying inconsolably. Her long, dark hair cascading down her face, hiding her from view. Peering round I hoped that I would lay eyes on someone who would be better equipped to deal with this situation than me! It's not that I'm cold hearted but the thought of having to deal with someone else's emotional issues is not my idea of fun. But sadly, there was not another soul in sight. Taking a deep breath, I pondered in my head for a second whether I should just tip toe back down the gravel drive and go on my merry way. But of course, I didn't. I couldn't. Call it a sisterhood calling or whatever you like but I had this overwhelming feeling to go and find out what she was so upset about, or at least stop the wailing with some calming words.

"Hello? Are you okay?" I cheerily called out, hoping that she was just having a bad day and I could just continue with mine, without getting too involved in a sob story. It's not that I don't care about others, but I just really didn't have time to get involved with other people's drama.

With her head down she didn't hear me when I called out, so I tried again a little louder and firmer this time. That worked! I may have shouted a little bit too firmly but like I said, I'm a busy woman.

Her head shot up and after quickly spotting me she pulled down the sleeve of her oversized cardigan and wiped her nose and eyes before jumping to her feet.

"Hi, can I help you?" She sniffed, doing her best to plaster some sort of fake smile across her pale face.

"Are you okay, I heard you wail.., I mean crying?" I asked, trying to sound at least a little concerned. The woman just stared at me and as I edged closer, I could see that her eyes were still brimming with fresh tears and that this was going to take a lot longer than I first anticipated. "So, what's up?" I continued trying to hurry things up a little whilst still smiling a sweet, albeit fake, smile. "Anything I can help with?"

And then she opened her tiny, perfect, little mouth and the words poured out, as did a torrent of heaving sobs

13

which intermittently broke up any sentences that I was desperately trying to make sense of.

"Okay, let's slow this all down, shall we?" I plead, my hands gesturing to her like she's a barking dog that needs to calm the hell down. I spot a shabby wooden picnic table on the lawn beside us and gently take her arm and guide her towards it. Fishing out some unused tissues from my denim jacket pocket I hand them to her and after a good nose blow she begins to calm down. Hoping the now even grottier looking bench is strong enough to take our weight I gesture to her to sit down.

"I'm fine, it's nothing really," she sniffs, gulping for breath still but definitely looking a bit more human now.

"It doesn't look like nothing to me." I grimace raising my eyebrows. "My name is Velvet." Holding out my hand towards her I introduce myself trying to relax her a bit so that she might say more than six words I can actually understand."

"That's a really pretty name." She smiles gently. "My name is Tiffany, and my husband has just left me!"

This could be a long one I think to myself. But I've started so I must finish and there was something about Tiffany that made me want to listen to her story. "What happened, if you don't mind me asking?" I continue, even though I can guess that the whole story will go along the lines of husband cheated with younger woman and has upped and left without even a second glance back at the destruction he has left behind. Been there, seen it and yes, I watch a lot of television shows!

Tiffany looks at me and after taking a long, deep, shuddering breath herself she starts to tell me how she had come home from work one lunchtime to pick up some files only to find her darling husband Travis had indeed found himself a younger woman. Her sister! No wonder the poor woman was sobbing, the carpet containing her whole world had well and truly been pulled from beneath her delicate little feet.

Her husband was one of the local doctors and by the sounds of what she was telling me, he had always been a bit of a charmer. I would imagine that Tiffany's sister was not the first to experience his wandering stethoscope.

I had been on the painful end of an unfaithful partner and I really did know how it felt to have your heart shattered into a million tiny pieces. And a million tiny pieces were what I had turned the windshield of his beloved car into when I found out what he had done. It was like a switch inside of me had flicked and a new side of me had been released and, my God it had felt so good!

I had been careful not to let him have firm proof that it was me who had battered the overpriced heap of junk into oblivion of course, but he knew it was me. He never reported me to the cops for doing it because I think he was truly too scared about what I might do next.

I had continued to chat to Tiffany for another good hour, trying my hardest not to look at my watch every few minutes and, after assuring me she was going to be okay, I went on my way. Sitting in my car, I had taken out my phone and quickly and efficiently found out where Travis worked. On my way home I couldn't help but drive by his doctor's office and pull up outside. Just at that precise moment Dr Travis Holboune, Doctor of Love and Destruction was heading to his black 4x4, whistling as he went, as though he had not a care in the world. A flash of anger kind of flared inside of me and watching as he reversed his car out of his parking bay, I decided to follow him. I had no clue what I was going to do and really Tiffany and Travis were nothing to do with me, but I felt a strange sort of need to make Travis pay for what he had done.

Travis didn't go far and it wasn't long before he pulled up beside a young, dark haired girl who was sat waiting on a bench. I knew in an instant that this was Tiffany's, quite a lot younger sister.

Keeping my distance, I watched as the two of them drove down the street and headed out of town. After about ten minutes of driving, they indicated and pulled into the driveway of a large new build house which sported a 'Just Sold' sign. It was obvious that these two lovely humans had been planning this for a while.

Swinging my car round in the street, I headed back home, a plan growing in my head.
In my younger, more wild days I had experimented with different 'substances' and still had a few contacts in the business. A quick phone call later, I had received what I needed and after night had fallen, I headed back to the good doctor's love nest. Luckily for me, in their excitement; the two lovers had forgotten to lock the car and in a split second I had done what I wanted and was on the way back home before anyone was the wiser.

The next morning, I made a call to the local police station tipping them off that I had seen a black 4x4 doing some dodgy dealings outside a local school and had given them the registration plate of Travis' car. The headline of the local paper the following week read; "Local doctor arrested for drug dealing."

Dear Travis, despite protesting his complete innocence, was given a Police caution and was struck off from his job. No one wants a druggy doctor treating them and Tiffany, as far as I knew, moved away for a fresh start a long way from here.

It felt so good to turn the tables on someone like Dr Holboune and although there might have been a twinge of guilt, it was hopelessly overpowered by a wave of satisfaction. My thirst for vengeance was well and truly ignited. It was just a shame that no one paid you to do this as a job…

Chapter Two

Can I just say that you can literally get paid to do anything in today's world and I mean anything!

I watched a news report once about a company that had made its fortune delivering bottles of water to office workers that were too damned lazy to get off their overpaid backsides to walk to the corner store to get one or the communal water fountain, down the corridor. The company had built an app where you just clicked and within half an hour, said bottle of water was delivered to your desk, all for the small fee of $6! What was even better was the company's idea was that it had been set up as a joke and had skyrocketed! All I can say is "Well done boys and girls, you deserve every cent."

Whilst watching the enlightening news broadcast, my eyes fixed on the screen while I fed myself handfuls of toffee popcorn, I wondered just how far people would go to get what they wanted without having to lift a finger themselves. Don't get me wrong my own little business was ticking along very nicely, but I never felt truly satisfied when I got home from work. Perhaps it was time for a change?

Flicking through the channels a little later in the evening, I came across a TV documentary about something I didn't even know existed... the dark web. Sounds spooky, doesn't it? I literally had no idea that beneath the glamour of social media and beautiful websites, lay a place where anything could be bought or sold pretty much without the authorities knowing about it. It is a world of dodgy deals, hackers and dark deeds where only the bravest or most desperate fear to tread. Anything from guns to drugs to hitmen could be bought, sold and hired; it was beyond fascinating and I was hooked.

But what the documentary didn't really mention, (well, either that or it came on when I nipped to the loo) was how you actually accessed the dark web. I really, really wanted to access it and I knew a man that might just help me with that: Tommo.

Tommo was one of the local drug dealers and before you gasp and think, "My God, what sort of neighbourhood do you live in?", can I just say that EVERY neighbourhood has a local drug dealer or two. It doesn't matter how posh you think your little suburb is, I can guarantee you that those yummy mummy friends of yours also need a little pick me up now and then and they will go to some pretty shady places to get them.

Now, Tommo always frequented a certain bar on a Friday night, well most nights to be honest, and, although you would class him as shady, he had never done me any harm. In fact, he had come to my rescue in my darker days. He was a fellow lost soul and he was my go-to person if I needed any help or advice.

We had met at a bar across town late one evening, when I was drinking myself into blackness just after my mother had died. It was his faint British accent that had snapped me out of my alcohol filled fog, and after we struck up conversation something just 'clicked'. It turned out he too had moved over the L.A. as a kid but a falling out with his family meant he too was now on his own. I didn't care what he had done in the past, I just knew from the moment we met that we would become solid friends.

I wasn't a drug addict, let's just get that clear and, it wasn't just hard drugs that Tommo could lay his hands on, it was also a few prescription ones too. I had only ever taken a little something when I felt my world was becoming a bit too heavy to bear and could go months without needing some medicinal help but knowing that Tommy had something to ease away the dark clouds was almost a comfort. Hard drugs like heroin and cocaine are something that I have never touched, for the one reason that I did not want to become slave to a chemical. I have always been my own person and that is how it will always stay.

Tommo was in his usual dark corner chatting to a bald-headed guy wearing round, mirrored sunglasses. I will never understand why people wear sunglasses inside dark bars but I'm assuming it's so they aren't recognised? To me it makes you more conspicuous as I immediately think "Why the hell are you wearing shades in here?"

The minute I walk over to Tommo, the bald guy pops up like I've trodden on his activate button and slinks away into the gloom of another corner. Swinging my fake leather trouser-covered bottom into the seat next to Tommo, I clink his glass with mine.

"Evening Velvet, what can I help you with tonight?" Tommy sighs, taking a long sip of his beer.

"I want to know how to get on the dark web," I whisper, casting my eyes about for any CIA agents that might be lurking and listening in on our conversations.

"The dark web? What do you want to go on there for then?" Tommo laughs loudly before I shush him. "What sort of flowers are you trying to sell?" He winks, still chuckling.

"I'm just curious that's all." I reply, putting on my sweetest smile and battering my eyelids just a little.

"It's not a place for a girl like you." Tommo continues, giggling still. "There are things on there that would turn your blood to ice, trust me."

"Please Tommo." I pester. "You owe me for helping you with the cops last month if I remember rightly?" my voice is now a bit firmer, and Tommo starts to shift in his seat.

Last month the bar got raided by drug enforcement and if it hadn't been for me creating one hell of a distraction, Tommo would be behind bars by now. Let's just say the said distraction involved a quick one worded text to Tommo and me pretending my van had broken down in front of the convoy of undercover cop cars that were streaming down the back alley to the only entrance of the bar. I had spotted the cars as they entered the main street and my gut instinct told me where they were headed. I had managed to slip in front of them a couple of cars ahead by nipping down a side street and after fumbling the word COPS to Tommo I preceded to slow my van down to a jerky crawl.

The cops were soon tight on my rear bumper as I revved the engine to create a cloud or two of black smoke which I hoped by some magic would look convincing enough to stop me getting arrested. With hazard lights on I slunk to a stop and stepped out to lift the bonnet and was soon joined by a broad shouldered, shaven headed undercover cop who insisted very firmly that I got back in the van sharpish while he and another uniformed cop pushed my van to the side of the street. He was pretty pissed, of course, but I apologised and played my trump card of being a blonde bimbo and they went on their merry way. Luckily, Tommo had received my text and was long gone by the time the cops kicked the door in. He really did owe me big time and I wasn't going to let him forget it!

"So come on, help me." I grin, drumming my hands on his skinny thigh until he bats me away like an annoying fly.

"Okay, okay." Tommo sighs, rolling his eyes skyward as he downs the rest of his drink. "But I will not, in any way, be held responsible for any trouble you get that pretty little head of yours into, right?"

"Cross my heart and hope I don't die." I smile, a twinge of hesitation loitering in my head as I worry if this was such a good idea.

Just under an hour later Tommo has downloaded a special app onto my phone, shown me the way into the dark web and I now already feel like a criminal (but I quite like it!). There are quite a few things to negotiate before you can access the dark web and I'm not the savviest when it comes to computer technical things, but I am determined to learn. As we dabble on the dark side, both squinting at my phone as its screen illuminates our determined little faces, I wonder where I can find adverts for hitmen. It's not that I want someone dispatched, it really isn't, I just want to see how they word their adverts, so to speak! Do they just say at the top 'Hitman for hire'? Do they have a price list? A choice of ways to do the deed? I have so many questions and I'm not sure Tommo can or will answer them all. But I really don't want to involve anyone else. My trust levels are pretty diminished these days and I like to keep my circle very small. I will just have to work this out my own way and I'm pretty sure there's a You Tube video on it…

***

Tommo is right, the dark web really is not for the faint hearted, and after a few minutes I am even more intrigued than I was before. It's not all scary stuff. A lot of it is just really, really weird and I can feel myself getting a little bit addicted to what I'm seeing. I can feel Tommo's eyes boring into my illuminated, fixated face. I dart him a sideward glance.

"What?" I smirk, knowing full well that Tommo is now really regretting helping me access these kinds of websites.

"You are making me very nervous, Velvet," Tommo grunts, his eyes narrowing as if he's trying to work out what on earth I have planned that involves the dark web. "Before I help you anymore, I want to know what you've got planned."

I pause for a second; I need to keep what I have got planned very hush hush but I also need to keep Tommo onside in case I need some help with this dark web stuff later on.

"Okay, okay, let me go get us a couple more drinks and I will tell you my idea, but you have got to promise not to laugh, alright?" I wink as I ease myself up from the table and flicking my curly locks over my shoulders, I prance to the bar grinning like a Cheshire cat.

Ordering two bottles of beer and a couple of Old Fashioneds to keep us going. I spin round and lean my back against the bar while our drinks are sorted by Tony, the barman. The bar is pretty busy tonight and in the low lights I make out a fair few familiar faces. But there are also a couple of guys I don't recognise and, as I accidentally allow my glance to linger a little too long on one of their faces, eye contact is made and he immediately springs up and sidles over. Great!

"Hi, I'm Jerry." The guy grins creepily as he eagerly wipes his hand on his trouser leg and holds it out for me to shake.

I reluctantly take his sticky hand and shake it briefly before letting it drop. "Hi Jerry, nice to meet you but I'm with someone." I grin back before turning my back on him to collect the tray of drinks Tony has left for me.

"Now, come on, I'm sure a pretty girl like you wouldn't give me a look like that if you weren't looking for someone to share those drinks with." Jerry creepily whispers in my ear, the smell of stale liquor wafting through my hair.

I can feel myself getting angrier by the second and as I feel the delightful Jerry press himself up against me a little more I decide it's time to end this little situation before it gets out of hand. Swiftly bringing my leg up behind me, I plant my heel clad boot firmly and accurately into his groin and as he crumples into a heap behind me, I know that I must have applied just the right amount of pressure.

"You nasty, teasing bitch," Jerry spits, writhing on the floor as I carefully step over him with my tray of drinks held high.

Behind me I can hear dear Jerry being helped to his feet and propelled out of the door by Tony and I make my way back to Tommo who is disapprovingly shaking his head at what he has just seen.

"What?" I laugh, as Tommo takes one of the bottles of beer and takes a long swig from it.

"You, Miss Darke, are like no other girl I have ever met," he chuckles.

"Us girls have to learn how to take care of ourselves against creeps like that." I shrug, adjusting my jacket as I sit back down next to him.

"Oh, I can see you are quite the master in that art." Tommo continues. "Now please tell me, what on earth you have planned for all this dark web education? I am totally intrigued."

While we sip our drinks I fill Tommo in on what happened when I met Tiffany and what I ended up doing to Travis.

"Are you completely insane?" Tommo coughs, choking on his beer as I relay the story to him. Tommo is the one who had supplied the drugs to me I just didn't tell them what they were for."

"He deserved it," I reply simply, a smile creeping up one side of my lips.

"Well, yes it does sound like it, but was it really your revenge to take? What do you get out of it?" he hisses.

"I got a great deal of satis-bloody-faction actually and that is why I want to go on the dark web. I think I could make a living out of taking revenge for people who have been wronged." I beam, leaning my chin on my hand as I study Tommo's face for his reaction.

Tommo just stares at me, not saying a word. He downs his Old Fashioned in one and shakes his head as the whiskey hits him hard. "You really are crazy!." he mutters, but taking my phone he starts tapping on the screen and in a few seconds, he hands the phone back to me. "Start on here; it's the most likely place to find out if this mad idea of yours has any legs to it at all." Tommo sighs. He knows that I will go ahead and do it with or without him, so he thinks he might as well help.

"What is this site?" I ask puzzled, as some of the threads of the page he has put me on seem to read as gobbledegook.

"It's mostly code for what people are after, services-wise. That's why it reads funny." Tommo explains. "Obviously you can't just put an advert out there asking for someone to bump off your ex-wife, for example, as the feds would be straight on it."

"You have to be clever and let people know what you're offering, but secretly, if that makes sense?"

"So I need to make a code of my own? What about my own separate website?" I ask, my head swirling with ideas.

"You really are deadly serious about this, aren't you?" Tommo sighs knowingly, tipping his head back to stare at the ceiling.

"You don't think it would work?" I ask him, pouting slightly.

"Oh yeah, I should think you will be inundated with every whacko in the city and beyond." Tommo laughs nervously. "Velvet, this little enterprise of yours could be very profitable but also very dangerous. You would have to pick your clients very carefully and make sure you aren't the one getting hurt."

I pause for a second picking at my nails as I process what Tommo is saying, but my mind is already made up. "I really think I could make a lot of money out of this and, of course, I know the dangers but like you've just witnessed, I can take care of myself pretty well. I just need to drum up some customers and in this city I don't think that will be too hard!" I grin, downing my own glass of Old Fashioned and wave the empty vessel in Tommo's direction. "Another one?" I wink.

Tommo looks me straight in the eyes, studying them to see if this is all just a wind up.
"Just one more, then. I've got my own work to do." He sighs, shaking his head wearily, but I can tell he is pretty intrigued by my idea.

"Just one more, I promise." I smile, catching his glass as he slides it across the table to me.

We both know it won't just be one more. I want to find out everything I can about the dark web and how I go about getting my own customers. Tommo will be fine all the time the free drinks are flowing. He clearly knows a whole lot more about the dark web than he is letting on and I want to know everything there is to know. I bet he even knows of some potential clients.

Chapter Three

Opening the shop at 8am the following morning the bright sunshine makes me wince. The just one more drink as predicted had turned into four or five, I can't be sure, as I lost count. But Tommo and I made good progress in putting together my little business plan and he promised he would help me find my first real customers, although I think he just told me that so I would go home.

The shop is starting to run low on stock so a trip to the flower market tomorrow is a must. Dragging out the last of the bunches of roses in their galvanised, water filled buckets I line them neatly outside the shop: the yellow ones are my favourites. There is one particular one called 'Penny Lane' and its intense colour just glows against the cold, grey sidewalk like a little pool of sunshine. It's just beautiful.

"Good morning, Velvet," a cheery voice calls from the little café next door. Mr Lin, owner of the café is out busily wiping and cleaning around the chrome-coloured tables and chairs that he has positioned outside. He is the sweetest old man you would ever want to meet and we had both been frequent visitors to each other's businesses since I opened up three years ago. He has run The Kettle café for over 30 years and not much has changed in that time. He took over from his father and he hopes that one day his daughter Lucy will do the same.

Lucy is a shy girl who looks much younger than her 22 years. Her hair always covers her face and she wears these thick, black-rimmed glasses that seem to swamp her doll-like face.

Mr Lin moved from Korea in the 80's and married a local girl called Helen. Helen sadly died a few years ago, from a heart problem, and it's just been Mr Lin and Lucy ever since.

We have our own deal going between us. I provide tiny pots of flowers for his café tables and he provides me with lunches whenever I want them. When his customers remark on the flowers, he eagerly tells them where they came from and if I'm lucky a few extra customers step through my door.

My main source of income is wedding and funeral flowers and seeing as there is either one or the other going on it keeps me going quite nicely. Lily's has become a popular place over the years and I'm proud of what I achieved after my mother passed away. She had always suffered with chest problems and a nasty bout of pneumonia had been what had finished her off. She had kindly left me enough money to set up the store and it felt only right to call it after her.

Mr Lin and Lucy always seemed to have a bustling business too and were very well liked amongst the locals. We were lucky to live in a neighbourhood where people looked out for each other and although, as with anywhere, there were rough parts, on the whole, we had no issues, apart from the odd bit of graffiti.

One night I had forgotten something in the shop and had popped back at night to collect it, when I stumbled across a young lad, hood pulled up and spray can in hand, ready to let loose on the wall outside my shop's entrance.

"Are you any good then?" I asked him, taking him completely unawares and making him drop his can at my feet. He went to run off but when he went to grab the rucksack of spray cans he had left, he suddenly realised I was holding them. "There's no need to run. I just want to see some of your work." I smiled, holding out the rucksack. "This is my shop and I might have a job for you if you are talented enough."

The young lad eyeballed me for a moment before scanning his eyes around to make sure I didn't have someone waiting to jump him. With a huff, he pulled down his hood to reveal a head full of neat braids and then took out his phone from his pocket.

"My tag is Jada. I don't want no trouble, lady. I just want to show off my art work. There's nowhere for people like me to go and show off our skills properly." He shrugged, still looking nervously about.

After tapping his phone a few times he turned the screen round to show me some photos of his recent work and I was totally blown away. "You did these free hand?"

I ask, taking the phone from him, my eyes not leaving the illuminated images.

"Yeah, I'm self-taught." He nods coyly as he scuffs the floor with his foot.

"So what were you planning to spray on my shop tonight?" I probe. "Can you do flowers?"

Jada nods and taking back his phone he brings up another image of a jungle scene he had created on a train bridge. The detail is incredible, especially the intricate orchids he has done.

"You are seriously talented." I gush, as I soak up the images into my brain. "Do you fancy a commission job? Here inside the shop?"

Jada nods and I gesture for him to follow me as I unlock the shop and switch on the lights. At the rear of the shop is a pure white wall with some shelving units propped against it. I use the shelves to display vases and pots I have for sale but for a while I've been thinking that I need some colour on them.

"What do you reckon you could do on that wall?" I ask Jada, watching his face light up at the sight of the sizable canvas.

"Something very awesome." He laughs, rubbing his head, his eyes darting about as if he is painting with them.

"Well, why don't you go home tonight and sketch me some ideas and meet me back here tomorrow? I take it you are still in school?" I question. Jada is one of these kids whose age is hard to guess.

"Yeah, I'm in my final year, so I could come back tomorrow around 4pm?" Jada nods.

"Sounds good to me." I nod back and after a brief chat about what I'm after I watch as he heads off down the street, disappearing into the darkness.

A few days later I sit and watch in awe as Jada unleashes his creative flair upon my bare wall. The ideas he has come up with are breath-taking and it is hard to choose what idea to go with but in the end we go with a rose garden type scene complete with a central fountain and birds flying overhead. It was perfect.

Jada, or rather Julius as his mother calls him, had told me not to pay him anything for the work as he had been so pleased to be appreciated for once. I had given him a narrow-eyed glare and promptly shoved a hundred dollars into his jacket pocket, daring him to refuse it.

"Good work deserves a reward and I might need your skills again one day, mightn't I?" I tell him, firmly.

Julius thanked me another few times and then finally headed back home, leaving me to stare in awe at what he had created for me.

The mural still looked as fresh today as it did when it was first done, and customers were always complimenting me on it the moment they walked into the shop. The only customers who don't comment or even notice the mural are the middle-aged, balding, usually pot-bellied husbands. They waddle in looking for a last-minute bunch of flowers to give their overindulged wives. You can tell the moment they walk in that you are about to be drooled over and it's a huge pet hate of mine. I liken their stares to those of chubby children staring through a sweet shop window at all the expensive candy they cannot afford and really shouldn't eat. Just because I'm tall, blonde, single and working behind a shop counter doesn't mean that I am fair game to be leered over. If they are particularly vulgar, I double the price by way of compensation and to be honest they are so busy staring at my chest that I could charge them triple and they wouldn't notice.

Sometimes I think having a man of my own would help ward off these sort of customers but in a way they help to pay the bills and I have as yet only had to smash a vase over one of their heads. That's a story for another day!

Mr Lin always asks me if I'm dating, and he doesn't seem to understand that I am actually quite happy being single.

"You are very beautiful lady for someone," he chatters. "You should have a good husband to take care of you."

That always makes me laugh because the only person I trust to take care of me is me! Maybe one day my so-called knight in shining armour will walk in through the door and sweep me off my feet but unless he is actually wearing a decent set of armour, I really don't fancy his chances.

I got burned by a man who I thought loved me a few years ago and now my defences are well and truly up and bolted. I don't want to have anyone else to worry about apart from me and that's how I am happiest.

Everything I have built up is mine and I'm not up for sharing it yet. Who knows what the future holds but for now it's the 'Velvet' show and that's a one-woman event.

This morning is particularly quiet and I wonder if there is some sort of event on nearby which has taken the usual flow of people away from our normally bustling street. I take the opportunity to have a decent stock check and sweep up inside. As I'm reaching to take down some boxes from a top shelf, I hear the familiar "tring" of the bell above the shop door.

Dusting off my jacket I step out from the back room and smile at two well-dressed ladies as they potter around pointing and cooing at some beautiful blue vases I've got displayed in the corner.

"Good morning." I smile, as I carefully place the heavy boxes onto the countertop and dust off my hands. As they turn around, I recognise one of them and remember that she ordered wedding flowers for her daughter last year. "How lovely to see you again, Mrs Hill. How was the wedding?" I ask, hoping that it hasn't already ended in divorce.

"Hello, my dear, how kind of you to ask." Mrs Hill beams back as she shuffles over to the counter. "It really was the most magical day ever and perfect in every detail including your beautiful flowers."

"I'm so pleased to hear that." I smile happily; it's always lovely to have positive feedback from customers especially about wedding flowers. "What can I help you ladies with today?"

"Well, my dear, Mary here is helping to decorate the chapel down the street for her great grandson's christening and I told her the best place to come for flowers is here," Mrs Hill explains.

"Well thank you so much, Mrs Hill; that is really kind of you to recommend me. I'm sure we can sort out something between us and I will do an extra special price for repeat business, how's that?" I reply.

"Wonderful," Mrs Hill laughs and Mary nods happily before instructing me on the colours and types of flowers she is after.

During our conversation, Mary tells me how her other daughter Kitty has been left high and dry by her lowlife boyfriend and how she is helping to pay for the christening as her daughter's ex has refused to pay for anything despite being a very well-paid lawyer.

"Someone needs to take that man down a peg or two," Mrs Hill tuts, shaking her head. "She isn't the first girl he has done this to and I doubt she will be the last, sadly."

"Men like him never get what they're owed." Mary replied glumly, shaking her head. "I would pay good money to see him get his comeuppance."

"Is that right?" I smile broadly. "I think I might be able to help you there."

Chapter Four

Tommo still thinks I'm bloody nuts and, to be honest, I'm starting to think that an hour or two on a therapist's couch isn't such a bad idea! I don't really know what's come over me lately, but I feel like I'm buzzing, like I have a new purpose in life, to avenging those who cannot do it themselves and while I'm at it, get paid for it. Surely that's a win-win situation?

Mrs Hill and her friend Mary thought I was joking when I said I could help them get revenge on Kitty's ex and I literally had to gag myself to stop a torrent of over excited words spill from my overly flappy lips. I knew I had to pick my customers carefully and the whole idea of going via the dark web was that everything would be anonymous, but I just could not miss out on the opportunity of testing the waters with these delightful ladies. After all, they would be in as much trouble as me if anything were to happen.

It turned out that Mary had been quite a firecracker in her younger days and her eyes had literally lit up when I suggested I could honey-trap him and then leave him in, say, some embarrassing situation!

"Strip him naked and tie him to a lamp post as far as I'm concerned," Mary chortled, a real glow coming to her face. "Or perhaps lace his drink with something that will make him sit on the loo for a week?"

Jeez, Mary really was pissed at this guy!

"So what's his name and where would I find him?" I ask calmly, trying not to seem too keen.

"His name is Brad Harris and he works at Moby and Skreen, the big building just off Hollywood. He often drinks at a bar opposite called 'Jars'. That's where poor Kitty met him. Stupid girl should really have seen through the glossy exterior of that man, but sadly she didn't." Mary grumbled.

We had met the following afternoon at Mr Lin's café, after I had decided I needed an evening to either put a plan together or come to my senses and call the whole thing off. But of course, that wasn't going to happen as I already had a plan in my head for what I could do to dear Brad.

The Kettle café was fairly empty when I pushed open the frosted glass-fronted door, the coolness from the air con making my skin prickle slightly. Mrs Hill and Mary were already seated at a corner table wearing dark sunglasses, as if they were undercover. I chuckled to myself as I approached them but was grateful that they had heeded my words about keeping whatever we did under very tight wraps.

"Hello ladies, how are we?" I smiled, removing my own shades, in an effort to make them remove theirs and look a little less suspicious.

"Have you come up with a plan?" Mary whispered to me, her eyes scouting nervously about.

"Yes," I hissed back, trying to keep a straight face. I was betting this was the most excitement these ladies had experienced in a long time so I would let them continue for a bit.

We ordered some English tea for them and a cup of black coffee for me and after Mr Lin had kindly bought us a plate of delicious, complimentary, buttermilk cookies we started to talk a bit more seriously about what ideas we had all come up with.

Mary and Mrs Hill had obviously been doing a lot of planning, and judging by some of their ideas, I did start to wonder how bad a guy this Brad chap was and whether he actually deserved any of this. My strategy now was to perhaps stake out Brad in his natural surroundings and check out that he was indeed a bad egg. The last thing I wanted to do was hit on an innocent guy and look like a moron.

Our little meeting lasted just over an hour. To be honest the ladies did most of the talking and I just sat and listened, sipping my coffee, and nodding in all the appropriate places. I did explain carefully that I would want to suss out my target first and get the lay of the land before anything happened. This would be my code from now on I had decided, I would always check out what I was doing was more than justified and I would be safe doing whatever I was doing.

The ladies had agreed again to everything I was saying with lots of "Oh, yes", and "Absolutely!" They really did feel like a couple of aunts to me now and I wanted to do right by them. I still had a knot of doubt in my stomach as to whether I was right to be getting into this vengeance game, but there was something in my soul that urged me on that whispered to me to give it a go.

As I waved the ladies off down the street Mr Lin's daughter Lucy came out to clear away some cups and plates from the outside tables and smiled sweetly at me like she always did.

"Hey Lucy, how are you?" I asked her, not really expecting a reply as she was the sort that would just smile, nod and scuttle away rather than engage in conversation. I had the feeling she had lived a very sheltered life and from what I had learnt from her father, she hadn't had the best of times at school.

"Hi Velvet, I'm well, thank you. How are you?" Lucy smiled coyly whilst she gathered together the white crockery into her delicate little arms.

"I am very well, thank you." I nodded, but before I could ask her anything else she vanished back inside; she was a curious little creature and for some reason she intrigued me.

***

A couple of days later I was sat in my apartment throwing various outfits out of my closet in the general direction of my bed. Tonight, I had planned to visit 'Jars', the bar where my target, Brad, was likely to go after he had finished work. I had decided I wanted to blend in with the work crowd at the bar without looking too suited up. In the end, I went for the personal assistant look in a pinstripe, knee-length skirt, and plain white chiffon top. I added some dark-rimmed fashion glasses and pinned my hair up for the full office effect. Studying myself in the mirror, I grinned, I actually looked very convincing. I wasn't sure if I could pull off the shy office mouse vibe, but I would give it a go.

The door buzzer suddenly burst into life, making me jump slightly and I quickly stuffed a few essentials into a smart, oversized leather handbag and scurried to the door. Opening it slightly I put my hand over my mouth to hide the laugh that was about to come out.

"If you are going to take the mick then I'm going home," Tommo grunted. I had asked him along as my wingman and told him to dress like he was my boss. He only agreed when I told him that he might pick up a few extra customers at the bar.

Tommo had totally outdone himself; his normally wild hair was slicked back and he wore a dark blue waistcoat, jacket and trouser ensemble that made him almost unrecognisable.

"You look perfect!" I gushed, indicating to him to give me a spin so I could fully check out his new look. "Where did you get the clothes?" I ask him.

"Probably best you don't know," he half laughs, stuffing his hands into his pockets. "Shall we go?" Before I can answer, he hails a cab.

"Yes, boss." I laugh, saluting him and climb into the back seat alongside him.

As it's Friday evening the bar is brimming with loud, drunk, smartly dressed men and women and I worry I won't find my target very easily. I had taken the liberty of doing my research on Brad and found his profile both on local business pages and social media. I knew what he looked like, but in a sea of suits and slicked back hair it still felt like a challenge.

Finding a space at the bar I order us a couple of bottles of beer and we start to scan the crowd for Brad. It's not long before Tommo gives me a nudge and discreetly points at a table of four men situated at the back of the bar. Peering over, I scan their faces and bingo, sure enough, there's Brad. He is clearly the life and soul of the table and despite the noise of the bar I can pick out his booming voice.

"Let's go closer," I suggest to Tommo, but before he can answer, I'm off and luckily manage to secure a table a little away from theirs, enough out of the way not to draw attention to my snooping.

"Stop staring," Tommo hisses. "You need to be a little more subtle."

"Yes sir" I salute again, rolling my eyes as I swig my beer.

Taking out my cell I take a couple of sneaky snaps of Brad and his mates for more research when I get home, then go back to observing him. The talk is mostly of work, but it soon changes tone when a couple of smartly dressed woman head past, on their way to the toilets.

Without hesitation Brad leans over for a better view of their disappearing derrieres and the grimy comments start to flow between him and his comrades.

"He really is a slime ball!" I whisper to Tommo, who is obviously feeling completely out of place in these surroundings.

"Okay great, can we go now?" Tommo grimaces, his hands held in a prayer like stance.

"Just a little bit longer." I smile back giving him the same prayer gesture. Tommo just sighs and sits back, downing his beer.

What I want to observe really is how Brad reacts when the ladies come back out past him. Is he a total creep, or is he all bravado behind their backs? I think I already know the answer, but I want to confirm it. Turns out I don't have to wait long. As the same ladies come back out past the table, Brad stretches out a hand and takes one of the girls by the wrist.

"You weren't going to ignore me, were you?" Brad pouts at the girl, who immediately pulls her wrist away. "You ladies look like you need some company and us boys would love to buy you some drinks. What do you say?"

The two girls look each other and after a duet of "No, thank you," they march away, much to my amusement.

Brad looks immediately embarrassed and quickly and loudly calls "Bloody lesbians!" as they walk away, making his equally vile friends laugh.

This is one guy that does not like to be turned down and he is certainly making my skin crawl. Mary and Mrs Hill were quite justified in wanting revenge on him and I start to wonder how many other women have fallen victim to his 'Charms' and how many oats he has scattered across this city. Within a few minutes, Brad and his cronies are yet again drooling and being crude to another small group of young ladies. It seems he just can't help himself.

"Okay, I've heard and seen enough. Let's get out of here." I nod to Tommo and we drain our beers as one, slam them on the table and head for the door. Behind me I can still hear Brad gobbing off to his mates.

This is one job I'm going to really enjoy. Now I just need to work out exactly what sort of payback I can dish out. It has to be something safe enough to carry out, but with maximum impact.

Chapter Five

I am thinking that I need to keep things simple when it comes to Brad. It is all too easy to get over-excited and plan some elaborate revenge, but that starts to make things get too complicated and then there is more room for error. Plus, this is my first job, so to speak, and the last thing I want is to turn it into a complete disaster and embarrass myself completely. I've always like to have things planned down to the smallest detail and this is no exception. I can clearly see this guy deserves bringing down a peg or two and I want to make sure he doesn't see it coming. He should be fairly easy to target because the minute he sees a decent piece of female flesh, his brain activity appears to diminish instantly.

Brad seems to be a man of small needs: money, women and alcohol. I need to think of something that incorporates all three somehow. I will need to be very careful as, after all, this guy is a lawyer and will probably smell a rat if I am not very, very careful. For a whole week I take time away from the shop to learn his lunchtime routine and in the evenings I observe him as he prowls round the local bars looking for girls to leer over.

The trouble with Brad doing what he is doing with the women in the area, is that he is fast running out of those that don't already know of his sleazy reputation and I think that's my way in. Because I haven't really frequented these bars before, Brad has never seen me and therefore when I do step out into the same bar as him, I'm likely to look like fresh meat!

I already have a plan in my head and have all the tools in my handbag that I need. What I also need is a new look, as I don't want to be easily recognised by Brad or any of his lawyer friends in the future.

A short drive out of town is a costume shop called 'A Touch of Magic', run by a delightful older couple who happen to stock all manner of items from wigs to whacky costumes and props. The moment I stepped into the place I knew I was in heaven.

There were so many wigs and hairpieces to choose from that I literally couldn't make up my mind on which one to buy, so I ended up coming home with five! As I was paying at the cashier desk, I happened to notice that under the register was a glass cabinet that held packets of what looked like eyes. Crouching down I studied them out of curiosity and found out that they were actually coloured contact lenses. This was a whole new level of changing my image so, of course, I bought a couple of pairs of them as well. My own eyes are the most vibrant and distinctive blue and I would probably be easily recognised from them. Green and hazel brown were the two lenses I chose because I felt they would look the most natural when worn. I was lucky with my skin tone, with every wig I tried on seeming to look like it was my own.

I had planned to approach Brad in the bar the following Friday night and after digging through my wardrobe, I found the most perfect bubble-gum pink, knee-length dress, and a pair of shiny black kitten heels to complete my look. Coupled with a long, straight, dark brown wig and the hazel-coloured contact lenses, I barely recognised myself in the mirror! This was going to be fun.

A few nights later I was making my way up the sidewalk towards 'Jars' and, although a few butterflies started to fill my stomach, I was keen to get the show on the road. I had everything crossed that Brad was already there but nothing was guaranteed and tonight might not be the night. My plan of a sort was to sit at a table alone and act like I had been stood up by a date. Tommo had agreed under some pressure to again be my wingman for the evening, although his only job would be loitering at the bar, just keeping an eye on me from a distance in case I got into any trouble.

With a deep breath, I composed myself and pushed open the glass entrance door, the atmosphere was buzzing, and I instantly felt more relaxed. Slinking my way up to the bar and ordering a Margarita, I spotted a table that was about to become free. A young couple that had been sitting there had just stood up and were starting to pull on their jackets, so I hovered nearby with my drink. As soon as they walked away, I quickly slipped into one of the seats and placed my own leather jacket on one of the spare chairs. Scanning the room, I failed to spot either Tommo or Brad, so I wondered if this little plan of mine was even going to get started.

Pulling out my cell impatiently, I typed Tommo a quick message to ask if he was here already and within a few seconds he pinged back with a reply. *Just coming in the door*.

Sure enough, Tommo appeared at the door and as he put his cell away in his back pocket, he started scanning the room. As his eyes flicked from person to person, I could see he looked a bit puzzled and as he started moving around the bar and walked straight past my table, I suddenly realised that my new image had worked a little too well. Tommo hadn't recognised me at all!

Giggling to myself, I snapped a quick selfie and sent it to him and watched in great amusement as he stopped in his tracks and slowly turned around to look in my direction. He hurriedly typed a message back with just the words; *OH MY GOD!*

I was delighted because if Tommo didn't recognise me, then my hard work had paid off and I was ready to deal with Brad. Hopefully, all I needed now was for Brad to turn up and I could put my plan into action.

It turned out I didn't have to wait long. I was soon aware of Brad's booming voice as he strode into the bar, flanked by two of his slick-haired friends, like some royal prince. As they reached my table, I put my phone to my ear and pretended to be deep in conversation. I could feel their eyes look me up and down. When Brad was level with me, I flicked my eyes up to meet his and let a little hint of a smile creep across my shiny lips, just for a second. He responded with a wink and swept his hand through his floppy hair.

"Gotcha." I knew.

Continuing my phoney phone call with a dramatic "Stuff you!" Loud enough for Brad and his leering friends to hear, I slammed my cell down on the table and downed my drink in one before shoving it across the table for extra effect. I proceeded to dab my eyes with a serviette and sniff a little just to round it all off. I seriously should have been nominated for an Oscar.

Predictably, within a few seconds, I felt a figure loom over me and as I peered up, my eyes met with Brad's once again. There was no denying that this guy had an incredible presence, and he was good-looking in a sleazy car salesman sort of way. But there was also no denying that he did make my skin crawl and I was doing my hardest not to show it or choke on the overpowering wave of his aftershave.

"What's a pretty thing like you doing here all by yourself then?" Brad cooed as he dragged the spare chair into place beside me, span it round and straddled it. "Don't tell me you have been stood up?"

With doleful eyes I blinked a few times and nodded slowly. "My boyfriend is a pig," I sniffed.

"Well, how about I get you another drink and you can tell me all about it?" Brad smirked, placing his hand on my thigh, and giving it a squeeze. The urge to punch him square between the eyes was a strong one, but I forced it down. My plan was working beautifully, but I had to keep my cool.

A few drinks later, we were having a great laugh and Brad's hands were now doing a lot of wandering, so it was time for the next phase. Unbeknown to Brad, I had a high threshold for alcohol, but pretending that I was very tipsy was playing right into his hands.

"I need a man like you," I giggled, poking him in the chest. This only resulted in him trying to stick his tongue down my throat and with a quick evasion I dodged him successfully.

"I really need the bathroom," I grinned with a wink and as I stood up pushing past him, I grabbed hold of his tie, pulling him towards me so I could whisper in his ear: "Meet me in the bathroom in five minutes."

Brad could hardly contain his excitement and staggering my way to the bathroom door, I looked back and gave him another of my best winks and smiles. Hook, line, and sinker!

In the cubicle I rummaged in my handbag and pulled out everything I needed for the final phase. I could hear the girl in the next cubicle finish up, then head to the sink to wash her hands. Brad would be here very soon and I was ready for him.

This was it; my first proper vengeance job and I was determined I would carry it out to perfection. Hearing the bathroom door bang open, I stepped out of the cubicle and leant provocatively against it as Brad headed for me, unbuttoning his shirt as he went. Pulling him inside and slamming the door shut I allowed him to kiss my neck briefly, before instructing him to turn around and put his hands on the wall while I unbuttoned his trousers. Brad was loving it and obliged willingly, without hesitation.

"God, you *are* a little minx!" Brad panted in anticipation as I pulled his pinstriped trousers to his ankles, followed by his red, polka dot boxer shorts to reveal his fake-tanned buttocks.

It was at that moment Brad realised I had superglued his hands to the cubicle wall and panic set in. I'm not sure what brand of superglue I used but I can highly recommend it for strength and durability. To be fair, I probably didn't need the two whole tubes I used, but I wasn't taking any risks.

"What the hell have you done to me?" Brad roared, before I shoved a pair of black lacy underwear in his mouth.

"This," I whispered, "is for all those girls you have taken advantage of you disgusting pig." Throwing open the door, I adjusted my wig and dress and walked out of the bathroom, leaving Brad still firmly glued to the wall of cubicle. He was busily trying to spit out the pair of knickers and wrench his hands off the wall, both tasks were proving unsuccessful.

Heading back through to the bar, I gave Tommo a nod and he raised his bottle to me. We were out of here. A glance back over my shoulder made me grin as I saw a group of three women head into the toilets. No doubt in my mind that they would take a few photos and videos before giving Brad any sort of help. My work here was done.

After successfully hailing a cab, I jumped in and headed for another part of town. I had a spare longline t-shirt and a pair of leggings stashed in my handbag. A quick change in the toilets of a local store was all I needed to remove my wig and contact lenses and leave looking completely different, back to my normal, butter-wouldn't-melt, florist self.

When finally, back to my apartment, I slumped onto the couch and took a few deep breaths. I noticed my hands were shaking slightly while I tapped a message to Tommo to let him know I made it home safe. The shaking was a mixture of adrenaline and fear. If Brad had wanted to, he could have easily assaulted me, or worse, and that was something I really needed to consider for future jobs.

After a long, hot shower, I retired to the comfort of my bed and scrolled through some social media pages. As the screen brightened my face, a broad smile crept across my lips. On my cell screen was a post containing a heap of photos from 'Jars' and guess who was the star of them? Yep, you guessed it: Brad!

Apparently the Fire services were called to help remove Brad's hands from the wall of the cubicle and his bare-butt cheeks had gone viral! Plenty of women had come forward to share their experiences of Brad and offering to buy whoever did it some drinks. I felt like posting "No need to thank me." Hopefully Brad had been taught a valuable lesson with women and his pride had taken a huge hit. Such a shame.

***

The next morning when I opened up the shop, an envelope had been posted through the mailbox. Inside was a simple message.

'Dear Velvet, for a job well done.
Thank you.'

Also, inside the envelope, was $100. Mary and I had not really discussed a price for my work, being it was, my first 'job' but this more than covered it. I assume they had seen or heard what happened to Brad and were pretty happy with what I had come up with. Brad, on the other hand, was still probably highly embarrassed and still picking bits of cubicle wall off his hands. The wigs and contact lenses could be again, for future revenge work, so, not a bad profit for a first attempt.

It felt so good to think that I had helped set the world a little more to rights and I couldn't wait to find more work; I just needed to find a way of bringing clients in.

Chapter Six

Tommo and I had arranged to meet at a local burger joint for a 'business meeting'. I had promised him dinner in return for being my wingman on my first job, plus I also wanted to pick his brains again about my dark web website.

I had thought long and hard about what I could do and had decided that I wanted to keep with the theme of flowers. Everything I was offering to do had to be coded in a way that wasn't easily picked up by any authorities. So, I thought, by setting up a virtual floristry shop, clients could 'book' deliveries of certain flowers, which would be code for the service they required.

Tommo still stared at me like I was talking Russian as I explained my plan to him, but to me it made perfect sense. As we tucked into our towering cheeseburgers, I continued to reel off the various names of flowers and what they were code for.

For example:

- Black Tulips were code for mild humiliation such as leaving embarrassing objects on their property or cars etc. Clients could specify.
- Pink Peonies were code for something a bit more technical like, putting their email address or cell number on Craig's list or local notice boards advertising anything from sexual favours to free goats so they would get inundated with messages and calls.
- Red roses were code for honey-trapping, a bit like I had done with Brad but with either myself or someone else there to get any evidence on camera. Tommo just shook his head at that immediately, so I guessed I would need to work on him a bit more for that one!

Watching Tommo's reaction was enough to make me close my notebook. "What?" I asked exhaling loudly. It was like having an older brother telling me off for wanting to go to a party.

"Velvet, exactly how far are you going to take this thing?" Tommo asked, in between shoving French fries into his mouth.

"Who knows?" I shrugged. "Depends what the clients ask for, I guess. I wouldn't have thought people would want to take really nasty revenge on others, would they?"

"But what if the people you are being paid to humiliate or worse don't actually deserve it?" Tommo questioned as he sat back in the booth and studied me carefully.

I pondered that for a minute. Tommo was right, of course. What if people just wanted to be nasty for no reason? I would need to make sure that they were deserving of it just like I had with Mrs Hill and Brad. That would mean double the work, so any amount I charged the clients would have to figure that in too. It would also give me the chance to stake out the intended target and plan accordingly. There was so much to think about which that frustrated me slightly, but I was determined to make it work. There was definitely a market for this sort of work, I just needed to find the perfect way to tap into it.

Whilst I'm sat discussing tactics with Tommo, my ears pick up harsh words coming from the kitchen area. I can hear a woman's raised voice and a man shouting back. Within a few seconds, the swinging door burst open and a woman about my age storms through it, stops, yells some more whilst undoing her apron, and rolling it into a sort of ball, throws it at the male voice coming from the kitchen.

The woman spins back around and yells, "I told you, I quit!"

Our eyes suddenly lock for a second and I am left open mouthed. This girl, woman, whichever you class her as, is stunning. Her skin can only be described as dark caramel in colour and her eyes burn like amber. Long waves of shiny black locks are released from the neat bun on top of her head, and it cascades down her back like a tousled waterfall.

"What are you staring at?" she hollers at me, in a voice with an accent I don't recognise, and then continues to storm out of the door, slamming it hard behind her.

"Nika, get back here." A plump, balding man who has now appeared from the kitchen wearing a stained white apron yells after her. But it's too late. Nika has left the building and the street and it doesn't look like she is coming back any time soon.

"Who is she?" I ask Tommo, as I try and peer through the misted window to see where she went.

"How the hell would I know?" Tommo scoffs. "I don't know everyone in this city."

I tut loudly and losing sight of the mysterious Nika, I slump back down in my seat. There was something about that girl that left me wanting to know more and I didn't know why. She had a sort of beauty I had never seen before and she looked like she should have been on a Paris catwalk, not serving in a low-grade burger joint. Whoever she was, the mysterious Nika had vanished into the night, like a rare bird, and our paths were unlikely to cross again. Finishing my meal, I push my plate to the side and continue to write notes in my book.

"So what do I do once I have everything planned out? Who do I talk to?" I ask Tommo with a grin. I'm beyond keen to get my website up and running by the weekend and I just know Tommo will know someone who can design a dark web website for me.

Rolling his eyes, Tommo quickly taps his cell and scribbling a name and number on a spare serviette, he slides it across the table to me. "Tell them Big T recommended them." he nods.

"Big T?" I snort with laughter. "*YOU* are known as Big T?" This is too funny for words, but I can see Tommo isn't finding it quite as funny and I try to shift back to a straight face.

"Just call this number if you are serious about this whole thing." Tommo grunts unamused, crossing his arms defensively across his chest. "They will set up the whole website for you and have always been 100% trustworthy."

"Thanks so much again, Tommo, you are a true friend." I wink.

Folding up the napkin and placing it in my jacket pocket I leave some cash on the table to cover the meal and we head for the door.

Tommo bids me goodnight and as he crosses the street I can't resist and call out "Good night Big T."

Tommo flicks a finger back in my direction and shakes his head before he disappears up the opposite sidewalk. I shouldn't really tease him too much as he has been a good friend, but I just couldn't resist mocking him, just a little, over the 'Big T' thing.

Back at my apartment, I take out the serviette and read what Tommo has written.
It has the simple instructions - 'Nano Bites – 413 Junction Boulevard, ask for Petra.' I had heard of 'Nano Bites'; It was a gaming shop a few blocks down and although I knew of it, I had never stepped foot inside.

I needed to get everything I wanted down on paper before I met this 'Petra' and I was hoping that my potential new venture wasn't going to cost me the earth to set up. Scribbling away in my notebook, I tried to be as subtle, but as clear as I could be in what I was offering. I was paranoid at being arrested in my first week, so the website had to look like a totally legit business from the outside, I figured. Perhaps this 'Petra' would be able to help in that regard too?

***

The next morning I woke at 6am to visit the flower market. It was one of my favourite things to do as part of being a florist and I never tired of the early starts, knowing what would await me, when I stepped into the giant hallways that brimmed with fragrance and colour. It was like a sort of therapy, although you had to go with a tough shopping list of what you needed otherwise it was easy to get carried away, buying far too much of what you really didn't want.

I knew most of the vendors well and they were very happy to give me decent trade prices if I continued to buy from them each week. Roses were a huge seller for me and with Valentine's Day coming up in a couple of weeks, I wanted to see what was on offer. I liked to offer different coloured roses, apart from the traditional red ones and as I plodded down the aisle towards my usual seller, something caught my eye. In two large black buckets sat a rose I had never seen before. It was almost pure white, but the tops of its petals were tipped with crimson red. They were stunning. As I bent down to pick up a single stem, I twirled it slowly in my hand taking in its beauty. It looked just like it had been dipped in ink, but it was totally natural.

"In the trade we call them 'Blood Tipped Roses,'" a voice called out from beyond the vast array of roses and gypsophila.

"I've never seen anything like them." I reply to the trader, Karl. I have bought many different sorts of roses from him in the past, but none quite like these and I really wanted them. "I think we might have to do a deal on some of these for Valentines." I smile as he heads over to me with a pen and paper in hand. A few minutes later, I've placed an order for the following week and Karl lets me take the rose in my hand as a free sample.

With my small van loaded with what I need to supply the shop for the week, I head back to drop them off and set up ready to open at 9am. I was planning on visiting 'Nano Bites' in my lunch break and had carefully written up exactly what I wanted Petra to do for me regarding the website. I just hoped she didn't laugh in my face and think it was a ridiculous idea. Only time would tell.

Chapter Seven

I arrive at 'Nano Bites' just after 1pm and, with my carefully worded notes tucked safely under my arm, I pushed open the bright orange door and confidently stepped inside. The walls were stocked floor to ceiling with every conceivable game you would ever want to own and through the centre of the store stood units which housed demo versions of the latest gaming machines. Making my way to the counter, I noticed that the three guys playing on the demo machines were completely immersed in what they were doing. I figured a bomb could go off and they would still be sat there, controllers in hand, staring at the screen, without even blinking.

Reaching the orange Perspex desk, I was greeted by a chubby guy in a white Fortnite t-shirt and thick-rimmed glasses. He was busily eating handfuls of crisps out of an oversized packet and only put them down when he saw me staring at them.

"Sorry, that's my lunch." he muttered, slightly defensively. "How can I help?"

"I'm looking for Petra?" I replied, trying to act cool and nonchalant, all the time feeling my insides tie themselves in knots.

Nodding, he picks up the bag of crisps and sticking his head through to the back room, he calls out "Petra? Someone is asking for you?"

I hear a voice call out but can't make out what it's saying. However, the guy just nods and says "She's on her way." before he heads back out onto the shop floor and clambers into one of the spare brightly-coloured chairs to finish his lunch break.

I don't have to wait long for Petra and I hear her coming before I see her. Her boots make a clear tapping sound on the polished floor and the jangle of her heavily, jewellery-burdened wrists announce her imminent arrival. Petra's hair is pink and when I say pink, I don't mean pastel pink, I mean bright neon, doesn't-look-real pink. Maybe it's a wig, but I don't think so. A chain from her left ear connects to a nose ring and her eyes are heavily rimmed with black eyeliner.

"How can I help?" she smiles, chewing loudly on gum.

"Hi I'm Velvet. Tommo, I mean Big T, told me to come and see you about a website." I whisper nervously.

"You don't need to whisper, they've all got headphones in." Petra winks with a short laugh, nodding her head in the direction of the transfixed gamers. "What sort of website are you after?" Petra continues and I carefully place my note book on the counter.

"I'm starting a new business venture and I need to update my current website," I tell her calmly, hoping she won't tell me to get lost when she looks inside the note book.

Taking the notebook, she climbs up onto a round-topped stool and crosses her fishnet clad legs like she's about to read a bedtime story. I'm left standing there like a student waiting for their essay to be marked and, although I'm trying to act cool, I know she can tell how awkward I feel.

A few minutes pass and I gather the courage to speak and break the silence between us. "Does it make sense?" I ask her, bracing myself for her response.

Petra looks up and snapping my notebook shut, she makes her way over to me, ushering me closer with a neon clad claw like finger. "This is some seriously cool shit," she beams. "How did you come up with the idea?"

Flushed with pride, I give her a very brief run down on what had happened with Tiffany, obviously not giving out any real names. "So does this mean you are interested in the job?" I ask, with fingers crossed by my side.

"I cannot wait to get started." Petra purrs. "We need to meet somewhere a bit more private I think first, and I will show you some of my work, so you can decide what look you want. Then we can discuss the money side."

"That sounds good to me." I nod eagerly and scribbling down my cell number, I pass it across to her, but she shakes her head.

"You need to get a burner first." she replies. "If you want to do this, then you need to do it safely and so do I." Then, scribbling on a piece of notepad, she tears it off and hands it to me. "Message me on this number once you've got a burner sorted, okay?"

"Of course, yes sorry, I wasn't thinking." I babble and thanking her a few times, I head out of the store.

The 'Burner' she was referring to is an unregistered cell phone that can be used in situations where you don't want the number traced back to you. I was now feeling like a real criminal and although my heart was trying to beat its way out of my chest, an even stronger feeling of excitement was growing inside me again. Burner cells were easy and cheap to buy so getting one wouldn't be a problem. Hurrying back to my own shop, I stopped at a local tech store and purchased a mid-range one for $30.

My afternoon trade was pretty slow so, within a short time, the cell was set up and on charge, ready to message Petra. I just hoped she still wanted the website job but judging by her reaction to my idea earlier, I was pretty sure she wanted in!

Our first official meeting had been in the back room of 'Nano Bites', after closing time. I still felt, as I walked through the blackness of the shut store, that I would be arrested for even thinking up my new line of work. It was too late now though, too many people were involved, well two of them, but I wanted to keep my circle small and tight. The fewer people that knew about my plans, the better in my eyes.

Petra had shown me a few of the websites she had created for people like myself, and I was blown away by the standard of her work. On the outside these websites looked like legitimate businesses, but when you knew what to look for, their darker side seeped out. I didn't ask too many questions on what the websites were actually offering - I didn't really want to find out!

***

Fast forward to a week later and the bespoke website that Petra had created for me was ready for launch. I hadn't laid eyes on what she had created in its entirety, but she had sent me screen shots of some of the early pages. We had another meeting arranged for tonight for her to show me how it all worked and for me to pay her fee, which was a little more than I was expecting. But, when you saw her work, you couldn't argue that it wasn't worth every cent. I was just praying that I would earn enough money back once it launched. It was a gamble I was willing to take.

Pulling up my van outside 'Nano Bites' I could see Petra inside with the crisp-stuffing colleague I had met before and as I was ten minutes early for our meeting, I waited in the van and watched the world go by. Los Angeles is like most cities there is always something going on somewhere. This particular street was a mix of nail bars, cafés and thrift stores and of course the gaming store I was parked outside. This evening was a particularly chilly one and I watched as a homeless guy, dressed in an oversized and heavily torn poncho, wheeled his wonky shopping cart up the street. He headed down an alleyway, obviously looking for somewhere to settle down for the night. His cart was laden with everything from clothing to empty buckets and I often wondered how people like him had ended up on the streets. Was it by choice? Or rather was it a result of bad choices in life? When I see people getting by, with the minimum of things, it makes me feel very grateful for what I have: a good business and a decent apartment to call home. I really don't want to lose either and as I sit here thinking about what I'm about to do as a side-line, I again start to doubt the life-choices I am now making.

But it's too late now, Petra is tapping on the window, her vibrant pink hair glowing against the darkness of the street outside. Giving her an energetic thumbs up, I grab my things and follow her into the store, and she locks the door behind me. The shutters are down, covering the windows and I feel slightly trapped.

Petra's laptop is set up on the wide wooden topped table in the centre of the room, glowing like some portal to another world, and she gestures to me to sit down in front of it.

"Okay, so I really hope this is the sort of thing you wanted, and I obviously can change parts of it and how certain things work, but I think for starters this is perfect for what you need," she explains.

"What is the website called and how do people find it?" I ask Petra, too eagerly, my eyes not leaving the screen as images start to load on it. She had asked me for a selection of words that she could use to find a domain name and I had sent quite a long list, so had no clue what she had finally settled on.

"I kept it simple. People like something simple that they can remember," Petra replied leaning over my shoulder to tap a few keys and I unexpectedly catch a waft of her surprisingly girly perfume, which doesn't quite fit with her punk look. The screen illuminates even brighter and when Petra brings up my website, I feel the familiar knot of anxiety tighten inside me. What if I really hate it? What if this is all a horrendous idea after all? But I needn't have worried, the website, *my* website is perfect. From the background photos to the colour scheme, Petra has, of course, nailed it all.

'Black Blooms'

The name is short, but ideally suited. Suddenly my worries have vanished, and the spark is burning again in my eyes as I take in the layout and click on different parts, to see where it takes me. Any doubts I have float away.

"See? Nice and simple. Memorable." Petra replied and with another few clicks, she brings up the store page and shows me how someone would go about ordering.

It all seemed crazily easy and simple, and she explained that any payment through the website would be diverted into an untraceable account, to which only I had access. I felt like a gangster, again the reality of what I was setting up began to creep up my spine.

"Do you think this is safe?" I asked Petra. "I mean, the jobs I'm offering to do?"

Petra pulled up a spare stool next to me and started to roll a cigarette in her talon like fingers. "What you are offering to do at the moment, is very small fry compared to what else is on the dark web." She laughed, sealing the rolled cigarette with a swift lick of her pierced tongue. "There are literally hundreds, if not thousands, of websites out there offering to do prank calls, or send exploding glitter parcels through the post to people, as a joke and all you're doing is offering a service a few stages up from that. Plus, if you're offering to right a few wrongs in the world, I think your services could be very valuable to people not courageous enough to get their own justice."

I nodded enthusiastically and went back to my website. It wasn't like I was selling guns or drugs, or actually offering to bump people off. I was just a link between my potential clients and the doing of rightful vengeance.

***

An hour later and I am back in my van with a renewed sense of purpose. Although I'm a few hundred bucks lighter, I feel it will be worth every penny. Just as I'm about to pull away I spot a slightly drunk guy stumbling down the pavement, then stopping in a doorway and gesturing. I couldn't quite see what was going on but gut instinct told me to get a closer look, so I eased off the parking brake and let the van roll down silently, towards where the drunk guy was stood.

To my horror, as I got nearer, I realised that the homeless guy I had seen earlier was sat in the doorway of a thrift store and was being tormented by this other, inebriated guy. Checking around, I noticed that apart from me, no one else was about to step in and the cops would probably not be interested in a homeless guy getting hassled. I had to do something and opening my van door, I stepped out hoping that the drunk guy would see me and push off. Sadly, he took no notice and as I approached the doorway, I saw to my complete disgust, that this disgusting individual was now urinating on the homeless guy's belongings, whilst he cowered in the corner.

I'm not entirely sure what happened next, but it was like a switch inside me had been flicked and my anger boiled over.

Kicking out the guy's legs from behind, he toppled forward and fell flat on his face in a lake of his own steaming urine. Leaping on his back, I held his face down and whispered in his ear through gritted teeth:

"Scum like you don't deserve to walk this earth or breathe the same air as us normal humans do. I really hope you like the taste of your own piss." I spat. I could feel the veins in my head bulging and for a second, I felt completely out of control, but oddly in control at the same time. It was the weirdest feeling I had ever experienced.

"I'm sorry, I'm sorry," The idiot drunk guy gasped as he tried to lift his head, but with adrenaline pumping through my veins I was stronger than usual, and I forced his head back down.

The homeless guy had grabbed his stuff and, scurrying to his feet, he bolted down the street, only looking back briefly to blow me a quick kiss of gratitude, before vanishing into the darkness.

Turning my attention back to the scumbag that lay beneath me, I fumbled in his jacket pocket for his wallet. A quick glance at his driver's license told me his name was Todd and that was all I needed to know.

"Okay Todd," I hissed into his ear. "For your sake you'd best run when I let you up and not look back. I now know where you work. They will find out exactly what you have done, and I doubt you will have a job for long. Am I clear?" The guy nodded quickly and let out a whimpering apology from his position on the floor.

I, of course, didn't have a clue where this numbskull worked, but he didn't know that. Plus, he was highly unlikely to go the cops and report my retribution when he was dripping in his own urine.

Releasing his head, I leapt to my feet and as the guy got to his feet, he ran blindly into the night.

I wiped my hands on my jeans and just as I was about to get back in my van, I heard a slow clapping sound coming from up the street. Out of the gloom, into the dull glow of the streetlight walked Petra, wearing a huge grin and nodding.

"You, my friend, are pretty badass!" She laughed as she took a large drag of her cigarette, before blowing the smoke into the night air.

"Thanks. I don't know what came over me but I couldn't just stand by and watch that happen." I shuddered, the chill of the night now encasing itself around me.

"There needs to be more people like you." Petra smiled and with a salute she span on her heels and headed back to her store.

Chapter Eight

A few nights later, I hovered with my finger over the magical key that would launch my website onto the dark web. This was it, the next big and final step to get my new business venture up and running. Petra had kindly altered a few little things for me and I now felt that I was more than ready to find a client or two, or rather I hoped they would find me.

The number of my burner cell was linked directly to the site and any messages that came through could be answered via it.

*Click****

Job done; I was now live on the dark web and I already felt like a criminal. Petra had assured me that the site was untraceable and I had no choice but to trust her. Sat, staring at my laptop screen and back to my burner cell repeatedly, I wondered how long it would take for my first job to come through? Perhaps no one would message and this would all have been for nothing.

I needed a way of getting word out about my new business venture, but how could I do that safely? Flyers? Business cards? Word of mouth? It was something else I had to consider, but for now I needed to sleep so I had a fresh head for tomorrow. I had a large wedding order to get ready and I wanted an early start. Things in the shop had become quite busy in the last few days and with spring right around the corner it was likely to only get busier. Perhaps it was time to hire some help?

I was sure a laminated advert in the shop window would probably be all I needed to catch the attention of any job seeking person walking past, so a few minutes on my computer was all I needed to print off an advert saying:

Vacancy available
Apply within
Flexible working hours and good pay

It was a basic advert but hopefully effective enough to entice a few people to apply. I just hoped that it wouldn't attract too many unsuitable job seekers and I wouldn't have to spend hours interviewing. I wasn't asking for someone with experience making bouquets as I felt I would rather teach them my own style and ways of doing things. I had built 'Lily's' up from nothing and was proud of what I'd achieved so, really didn't want someone coming in who would change the dynamics of how I did things. Don't get me wrong, I am always open to new ideas and opinions, but 'Lily's' is a special place, and my customers are more like friends now, which is how I would like it to stay.

All I needed was someone who could run the shop while I am out on deliveries, or do some deliveries for me. Likewise, if my new venture took off, I would need someone ultra-reliable, who could run things at short notice, and not ask why. I really started to wonder if my wish list was getting a bit too picky and that I would not find anyone to fit the bill.

***

A day or two later, while I was busy making an order of bridesmaids' posies, the bell on the shop door rang and I heard footsteps across the wooden floor.

"I will be out in a second," I called as I wrestled with some raffia to secure my floral creation and, wiping my hands on my apron, stepped out of the back room to see if the customer required help. What I wasn't expecting was to come face to face with the fireball from the burger joint, Nika.

A moment of recognition and silence passed between us for a couple of seconds and before Nika could open her mouth, I took a deep breath, smiled, and asked if she was here about the job. Nika immediately rolled her amber eyes skyward, as if waiting for me to tell her a flat 'No' after seeing her roar out of her last job, but I was about to surprise her.

"Well, I was here about the note on the window, but I guess after yelling at you the other night I best be on my way." Nika shrugged as she went to turn towards the door.

"We all have our off days." I grinned. "Do you have any experience in this sort of business?"

"Not really, no," Nika replied, a little taken aback. "But I am a fast learner and I'm not allergic to flowers."

Her comment made me laugh. "When can you start?" I grinned, holding out my hand to her.

I know it must sound crazy, but there is definitely something about this girl that intrigues me, and it almost feels like I've met her somewhere before. This may be a complete disaster, but I like to follow my gut instinct and taking her on feels like the right thing to do, although I may regret it later.

"I can start tomorrow?" Nika replies, a smile lighting up her face, even though she still looks a little awkward as she takes my hand and shakes it.

After a quick discussion of pay, we agree a start time of 8.30am and she sashays out of the door. Following her out I watch as she blows a kiss to the heavens as if thanking them for the job. Peeling the job advert off the door I screw it into a tight ball, slam-dunk it into the bin and head back to finish my wedding order. I have a good feeling about Nika and I really hope I'm not wrong about her. I guess I would find out tomorrow.

Just as I am finishing the last posy with a length of hemp ribbon, my burner cell pings into life and my heart skips a beat. It's a message from the 'Black Blooms' website and my pulse starts to race. Holding my breath as I open it, I prepare for what might be something horrible, but instead I just get a simple message asking to order a bunch of red roses. It still made me swallow hard though since this is my first dark web order.

All I needed to do now was find out a bit more about the person on the end of this message and double check that what they were wanting was genuine. I intended to be meticulous with researching every assignment and although I was feeling pretty excited about this first job, I have to keep things calm and business-like.

Quickly tapping a message back, I asked them to email details to a specific email address, that Petra had set up. The details included who the person the roses were for, why they deserved them and anything else that would help me carry out my job.

A few minutes later, an email pinged up on my laptop and it detailed, at length, the whole back story of how 'Jay' was keen to let his wife know that he was well aware of her affair with her boss. The email came with attached photos of both the wife and boss, details of where they worked, even some screen shots of the messages that had passed between them.

After reading and reviewing everything I messaged 'Jay' back and told him I would contact him in a few days with details for 'delivery'. Although everything seemed totally genuine, I needed to be 100% sure that his wife did deserve this, and I would need a day or so to check everything out. I really hoped that Nika was right about being a fast learner because I was going to be a bit busy for the next few days.

Nika had arrived, bright and early, for her first day at the shop. So early that she was there before I was. Her hair was fashioned into a long fish tail plait that trailed halfway down her slender back. She wore a soft half sleeve top and faded jeans that were tucked neatly into a pair of thick soled, black boots.

Catching me looking at her, she quickly asked "Is this okay?" pulling at her top.

"Oh God, yes, sorry its perfect. I will give you an apron to wear in a minute, but apart from that, I am pretty laid back as to what you wear, as long as it's appropriate." I smiled. "I'm sorry for staring but you look like you could be a model."

Nika's cheeks immediately flushed red and she giggled slightly. "I have done some modelling in the past, but I cannot tolerate the creepy men that are involved with it all." She shrugged. "The money was really good, but it's not for me."

"I can quite imagine," I nodded. I knew how creepy guys at the local bars could be and like I said before, even in my own shop sometimes when the overpaid husbands would come in for flowers for their over-indulged wives and mistresses. The extra creepy ones would always lean on the counter letting their eyes wander up and down me as if I were an item on display, while they told me how much they earned and what car they drove. I would nod and smile in all the right places, knowing full well they were trying to impress me and always knowing what line was coming next: "So do you have a boyfriend or husband?" I always replied with a "Yes" now as it was the quickest way to end the creepy conversation and get them out of the shop. Unfortunately, some of the guys were more persistent than others and those ones always got a little something special with their order. I would charge them extra and on occasions, whilst writing out the personalised cards to go with the flowers, I would slip in an extra card with a different woman's name on it. I can imagine the explosions I caused when the wives received the flowers and it made dealing with the creeps a little easier. Thinking about it, maybe a 'Revenge Artist' has always been my true calling.

After giving Nika a quick tour of the store and a flying lesson on the till. She helped me set up the buckets of flowers and bouquets outside the shop and I took her next door to meet Mr Lin and Lucy, treating her to coffee and croissants. Nika was a super-fast learner when it came to the till and I assumed it was because she had worked in a few places over the years. I hadn't asked her for a resume, and I didn't want to see one. You could tell Nika had had a tough time, but I was all for giving people a chance and there really was something about her that connected with me. Perhaps it was that we were very similar people, and I could see a lot of myself in her. I had never asked her age either, but I guessed we were similar in that respect too.

I was sure I would find all I needed to know about her as time went on and I was keen to learn about her roots and family, but for now we had a job to do and so far she had fitted in nicely. I was well aware she had a temper and I hoped we wouldn't clash too much in the future, as I was not one for suffering fools gladly. Nika might decide that the job was too boring for her and want to leave but for now hearing her humming away whilst de-leafing roses, she seemed quite content in her role.

Feeling my burner cell vibrate in my pocket, I left Nika to her work and headed into the main shop to check the message. It was from 'Jay' again, this time telling me that his wife was heading out this evening for a 'business meeting' at a local bar. I had asked him to let me know the next time she was going out under suspicious circumstances but hadn't expected it all to happen so quickly.

I replied saying I would be in touch shortly, once I had verified the job, so to speak, and then quickly googled the name of the bar. The bar in question was called 'Hal's Place' and was across the other side of the city. This might prove to be an issue with any jobs that I took on. It was all well and good using my van to go to this sort of work, but with 'Lily's Florist' emblazoned on the side, I was fairly recognisable. Taxis were, of course, an option but that would prove to be quite costly in the long run, and I needed some reliable transport to get to and from any jobs that came up; something that would blend in and not cost the earth to run. An idea suddenly popped in to my head and I told Nika that I was just popping out for a minute.

Mr Lin was busily wiping down tables when I popped back to The Kettle Café and he immediately asked if I had forgotten something from earlier as I was back so soon.

"I just wondered if I could possibly borrow your car tonight?" I asked with my sweetest smile. I had borrowed his late wife's small black car once before when my van decided to die right before a wedding delivery. Mr

Lin never went anywhere really and the car, for the most part, was parked at the rear of the café, gathering dust.

"Yes, yes, of course, Velvet. Do you have van trouble again?" Mr Lin asked, concerned for me as usual.

"Not as such, but I need to go somewhere tonight and my van is a bit too big to take. That is so kind of you, thank you." I smiled, patting his arm. He really is one of the most genuinely kind people I have ever encountered and a true friend. As he hands me the keys he tells me to use the car as much as I like as it will keep the engine running well.

I promise to keep the car clean and fuelled in return and although he shakes his head and insists it's not necessary, I tell him it's not negotiable and we both laugh. He knows how stubborn I am and after I thank him again, I head back to the shop to see how Nika is getting on.

Chapter Nine

I decided I had no need to put on my undercover attire for this evening's stake out because I would only be observing from afar and not interacting with anyone intentionally. I would just go in and have a casual drink at the bar and observe what went on between Jay's wife and her boss, nothing more. It was merely an information gathering exercise and I was hopeful it wouldn't take too long.

After showing Nika how to lock up the shop and waving her goodbye, I headed home to the apartment to get ready. It was hard to know what to wear out tonight, I wanted to blend in with the business crowd that frequented the bar, but also didn't want to look too casual. In the end I went for tight blue jeans, a white vest top and a camel-coloured knee length jacket. With a pair of black heels and my hair in a messy bun, I gave a twirl in front of the mirror and happy with how I looked, left to get Mr Lin's car.

Speeding along the freeway towards 'Hal's Place' I planned what to do when I got there. Jay had already sent me a heap of photos of his wife and her boss so I would begin scanning the place when I arrived and once I'd spotted my targets, I would try and sit as close to them as I could. I had thought about asking Nika if she wanted to come out for a drink but seeing as she had only just started working for me, I decided to keep things separate for now.

Walking into a bar alone always feels a bit awkward and I have a habit of pretending that I'm on a call when I walk into places like that as it feels like it gives me some sort of camouflage. Sounds odd I know! 'Hal's Place' is pretty up-market and the beautiful blue illuminated sign is easy to spot from up the street. Pulling the car into a free space, I sit and take a moment to look at the photos Jay has sent me, one more time. His wife is very beautiful and her long dark hair and large eyes lead me to think that she is possibly part Italian. I have no clue what Jay looks like, and I really hope he hasn't decided to come out to the bar as well. Of course, I have no way of knowing and he obviously has no clue what I look like either.

Stepping through the door of the bar, cell clamped to my ear, I scan the seating area, then head for an empty stool at the bar and order a mocktail from the heavily bearded barman. Sipping my drink, I pretend to scroll through my cell as I continue to scan the tables for Jay's wife and her boss, then suddenly I spot them. They have literally just taken their seats at one of the tables and are already holding hands over the table. These guys really don't seem to care and I can tell why Jay wanted something done to get revenge on his cheating wife.

Discretely, I snap a couple of photos of the pair in action and forward them to Jay. His response is instant and he tells me to go ahead with any plan I have. But there is something in the back of my mind that tells me there is more to this scenario than meets the eye, something that doesn't add up with Jay's wife and her boss. I decide to sit and wait it out at the bar until they are ready to leave, then follow them to see where they go next. I need to be 100% sure in my head that I will be doing the right thing and if that requires a little bit more effort, then so be it.

After watching the couple for half an hour or so, I watch as the woman gets up to go to the bathroom and I take the opportunity to follow her. Taking time to wash my hands at the marble basins in the bathroom, I watch in the mirror as Jay's wife begins to wash her own hands.

"Wow, I love your earrings," I gush to her as I clock the diamonds that dangle from her ears.

"Thank you so much. They were a gift from my husband for our anniversary." The woman smiles, admiring the earrings in the mirror.

"How romantic," I continue. "Are you here celebrating tonight?"

"Yes, we are, this is the place where we first met so we always come back here to celebrate each anniversary." She smiles, with a big happy sigh.

My head is now whirring, a slight sick feeling is beginning to brew inside me, and I force it back down. "So where did you get married? I'm sorry to sound so nosey but my sister is getting married next year and I'm so excited," I lie, hoping that the woman will show me some wedding snaps on her cell.

Just as I hoped, the woman pulls out her cell and enthusiastically begins to show me her screen saver, which clearly shows that the guy she is with tonight is indeed her husband!

Smiling and nodding I tell I her I must get back to my drink and she follows me out of the washroom and heads back to her husband, who greets her with an equally huge smile. What the hell is going on? I ask myself. This is definitely the woman Jay is claiming to be his wife and that is definitely her husband.

Things are starting to feel a bit weird, so I sit back at the bar and go back through the screen shots that Jay has sent me, supposedly of the 'affair'. Something very fishy is going on and I need to get to the bottom of it quickly. I decide to google the cell number that Jay has been using to send me messages and photos and although I am expecting to draw a blank I am surprised when a link to a Facebook page appears. This Jay is either really stupid or really crazy, and I'm starting to think he is probably a bit of both.

As his profile page loads, I suddenly find myself staring at 'Jay' or rather Jason Hardwick, if that, too, is his real name. Scrolling through his photos, I realise that all but three of the photos are of semi-naked women, or strange quotes and memes. There is something very, very wrong with this guy and it immediately dawns on me that this guy is not a disgruntled husband. In fact, I am not sure what he is. Whatever he is though, it isn't good, and I start to scan the rest of the customers in the restaurant after a dark thought enters my head, that this guy might actually be here watching.

I've been set up. I know that now, but for what reason? Thankfully, this Jay/Jason has no clue what I look like or who he is actually dealing with through the dark web, and that is to my advantage. Taking out my burner cell, I bring up his number and attracting the barman's attention, I tell him my cell has died and ask if I could use the restaurant's phone to make a quick call. The barman obliges and I quickly punch the number into the handset.

Holding my breath slightly, I wait for it to connect and then listen as it starts too ring. Swivelling in my seat I scan the bar again and almost immediately spot a guy sat at the very end of the bar take out his own cell. Oh Christ, it couldn't be?

I hadn't taken much notice of this guy before as I had been too busy looking at the other diners so had totally overlooked him. I wasn't even sure if he was sat there before because my head was spinning so much, I couldn't remember. Keeping an eye on this guy in the reflection of the mirror behind the bar, I watched as he looked at the screen puzzled and then answers. Hearing his voice on the end of the bar phone, I quickly end the call but keep the phone to my ear, pretending to have a conversation with someone.

"What the hell do I do now?" I think to myself. This guy is clearly some sort of stalker and I need to warn the woman and her husband without drawing any attention to myself. I need to think fast and get out of here. I also need to get rid of my burner cell ASAP, before this nutter rings me to see who I am. So, I quickly, and carefully, slip t it over the bar top and drop it into a jug of water and lemon slices that's sat the other side, before anyone sees.

Getting the barman's attention once more, I hand him the bar phone back and ask for a pen and paper to which he grins widely and gives me a wink. Great! Now the barman thinks I'm going to give him my number! I really need to get out of here and fast.

Scribbling a quick note, I gather my things and head out across the main restaurant, past the woman and her husband who are sitting gazing lovingly into each other's eyes. The woman looks up and catches my eye for a second and I smile. Carefully, slipping the note out of my jacket pocket, I drop it neatly at her feet, then, pretending I have something in my shoe I stop and adjust it before pointing to the note at her feet.

"Oh, it looks like you've dropped something." I point and smile, leaving her to pick it up off the floor. I head calmly out of the front door and back to the car, my heart racing.

Sliding into the driver's seat, I start the engine and pull up slowly outside the restaurant, praying that my note is enough to warn her, but not implicating myself in any way. My note simply said:

The guy at the bar in the dark red jacket has been taking photos of you on his cell all evening. Looks like he is uploading them online! CALL THE COPS.

From my viewpoint, I spot the woman's husband at the bar challenging Jay/Jason and seconds later it has broken into a full-on brawl. That wasn't exactly how I had planned it to go but, hearing sirens in the distance, I knew that the staff had called the cops and that was my cue to leave.

With my heart still pounding I drive back towards my own part of town and to the safety of my apartment. I am going to have to seriously re-consider this new line of work because I really don't want to be in that sort of situation again. I knew there would be risks and Tommo was right, it could become dangerous, but I didn't expect it on my first dark web job. Dialling Tommo's number, I wait for him to pick up.

"Where are you?" I ask him, still sounding a bit breathless.

"My usual place," Tommo replies, "You okay?"

"Yes…. No…. well not really, I will explain all when I get there." I sigh, ending the call.

I know exactly what Tommo will say, but I need to talk to someone I trust, and I need to do it tonight.

Chapter Ten

Tommo's response when I blurt out the whole Jay/Jason story, over several bottles of beer, was more sympathetic than I imagined. He did, of course, give me a bit of the old "Told you so." But on the whole, he calmed me down and made me think logically about it.

Like he said, had I not taken on the job and cased out this couple at the restaurant and done some groundwork, I would not have been able to alert them to the weirdo stalker and God knows what might have happened. Hopefully, now said weirdo was locked up he would stay that way and I had probably saved the cops a bit of work in the future.

Returning home that evening I definitely had a bit more of a spring in my step but there was still an itch at the back of my mind, causing me to doubt what I was doing. But I am not one for giving up and now I felt like this new role had new purpose. Could I now be in a position to right some wrongs in a different way, like I did tonight? We would see. For tonight, I was just happy that this evening's adventures had actually worked out okay. Even if I hadn't earned a penny from it.

It would take some time and experience to get things running as smoothly as possible. As long as I expected the unexpected and kept my wits about me, I was sure it would be alright. With Nika now helping out in the shop, it would allow me to make some extra checks, before heading out on any more jobs. If I actually got any more! Perhaps this would be my one and only semi disaster of a job via the dark web and I would have to go back to being a full-time florist and pack my wigs away.

***

Nika was, as usual, punctual to the second every morning and had continued to take to her new role with great enthusiasm, even suggesting new ideas for bringing in more customers. We had developed quite a bond over the last couple of weeks and despite her prickly exterior, underneath lay a warm-hearted soul, so I was keen to know her back story. I had tried to slip in a few questions about her family, asking where they were from and did they live locally, but the minute I mentioned anything, Nika changed the subject. She was clearly trying to avoid the conversation and I got the hint that I shouldn't push her too much. That was fine by me because, after all, she had never really asked me about my family, apart from asking about the name of the shop. Nika had clearly lived in LA for a while, if not grown up here, as she knew the area like the back of her hand, which was perfect for deliveries.

My second dark web order had come though at 2am one morning, a week or so later. I was almost nervous to open it in case it was a pissed off Jay/Jason again, but this person appeared to be totally different. Petra had shown me how to check IP addresses and this person seemed to write in a different way too, but I still proceeded with extra caution just in case.

The email simply requested 'Black tulips', which were code for mild humiliation. The accompanying special instructions asked for the 'tulips' to be left on an expensive car that belonged to a husband, who sounded like he had been a bit of a naughty boy.

Having bought a sparkly new burner cell and with a promise to Petra that I wouldn't dump this one in a jug of water so hastily, I awaited the details of my next job. It was obvious when the text came through that this guy had seriously upset his wife, but she still clearly loved him and only wanted to give him a bit of a fright, so to speak.

The car in question was a stunning, bright red, Mustang Coupe and the disgruntled wife wanted me to do something to the car to make said husband aware that his extramarital affairs had been rumbled. By the sounds of it, this hadn't been his first strike and I wondered why on earth you would stay with someone who repeatedly cheated? But hey, this was her choice and if she was willing to stump up some money to see it done, I wasn't going to say no. The beauty of the Black Tulip jobs were they caused no real harm and didn't need much checking out beforehand. All I wanted to be sure of was the location of the car at a certain time of the day, which the client had kindly already notified me of, and I was all set.

Taking into mind that I might well be being watched or set up, I did a few days of drive-bys of the car and waited until the early hours, one morning a few days later, to finish the job. The car was beyond beautiful, and I couldn't bring myself to do it any real damage. So instead, I plumped for covering it in spray glue, a whole load of glitter and about 100 thongs! Yes, 100 thongs of every conceivable colour and size. Did you know you can get ten for $1 in some stores? An absolute bargain! The glue would, of course, take a bit of washing off, but there would be no real lasting damage.

Snapping a few photos from different angles, I sent them over to the client and, to be honest, it was the easiest $150 dollars I had ever earned. I would love a few more jobs like that and I even got to dress up in one of my new wigs, just in case I was spotted on CCTV. I might have to re-think the glitter though, as, my God, that stuff literally gets everywhere. Had someone shone a torch on me that night, I would have twinkled like a guilty Christmas tree!

My client was more than pleased with my work and promised to let a few of her close friends know about my services. She had even sent me a photo of the husband cleaning the car with a power washer, whilst she drank a cocktail. I'm positive he knew she was behind it, but what could he say really? Vengeance can be a beautiful thing at times.

A few weeks later and with about two dark web jobs a week coming in, I was making a nice bit of extra money on the side so decided I would start to invest the money back into 'Lily's', by way of the small apartment that was above it. It had been nothing but a storage room before for the shop but now, with the back room kitted out with proper shelving, it seemed right to make the most of the apartment and potentially move into it, instead of renting my apartment. It was always a job I wished I could get round to doing and now with extra money coming in and Nika helping in the shop, it was finally going to get the attention it deserved.

Living above the shop, would not only save me time in the mornings, but also help with security. Mr Lin and his daughter lived above their café so we would be true neighbours too. Everything was falling into place, and I wanted to keep it heading in that direction. So far, the new jobs that had come in had been straightforward, without a stalker or weirdo in sight, and that had helped me grow in skill and confidence for more complex jobs to come.

Petra and Tommo had both continued to be loyal friends and had, I am sure, nudged people in my direction. I probably owed them big time for all the extras they had done. Tommo was easy to please, with a few drinks out and a takeout, but Petra was not one for socialising, so instead, I would send over a box of Krispy Kremes to 'Nano Bites', which I knew she had a weakness for.

Renovating the apartment was hard work, but once all the old furniture and junk was out and the walls freshly painted, it all started to take shape. I had even sanded down and varnished the old floorboards, by myself, and found some bargain furniture at the thrift store down the street. Whilst clearing out my old apartment, I had come across an old black and white photo of my mother, in her garden, as a young woman. The photo was extremely special and always bought a lump to my throat, so I had it reproduced and blown up on a large canvas, which I had framed and placed on the wall behind the till in the shop.

Nika said that I was the image of my mother and although I could see some faint resemblance, I wondered if I looked more like my father. I had never met my father. He had been killed in a car accident before I was born, my mother unfortunately only had one photo of him. It wasn't until the day of her funeral that I discovered my father had been a married man and that he and my mother embarked on an affair for three years before he died. I honestly don't think he knew my mother was pregnant at the time he died, and I was a true secret baby. My mother's family had been very clear at the funeral that they wanted nothing more to do with me. I was an outsider to them and a veritable blot on their perfect family vision. So, without saying a word to any of them in reply, I walked away. My heart had felt like it had turned to stone, feeling like I had nothing and no one was hard to take, and for a while, I went off the rails.

Arriving at the lawyer's office for the reading of my mother's will, two weeks later, I looked like I had been living on the streets. I had lost all respect for myself and had I not happened to meet Tommo back then in the bar, I would have certainly ended up homeless, or worse. He had taken pity on me and offered me a couch for the night. I knew he was drug dealer, so must have been crazy to take up his offer, but I was desperate and really didn't care what happened to me. Like I said before, we just clicked and I trusted him.

When the lawyer read out that my mother had left me a sizeable lump of money in her will, I was stunned, and judging by the look the lawyer gave me over the top of his steel rimmed glasses, so was he. I could have taken the money and drank or abused it away, but for me it had been a turning point. Leaving the lawyers office in a bit of blur, I happened to walk past an empty store with a 'For sale' sign, stuck in the window. I called the number, arranged a viewing and within a month 'Lily's' was born. My own business, named after my beautiful mother and a positive 'Up Yours!' to her family, who had abandoned me. The greatest revenge is success, I worked my backside off to make 'Lily's' the profitable business it is today, and I was damn proud of myself.

I often wondered about my father and who he really was. My birth certificate had the name Edward Hopkins on it, but with it being quite a common name, I came to a dead end trying to trace any relatives on his side. I didn't push the search too far as I felt like I might get the same reaction from his family as I did from my mother's and probably even a worse one seeing as I was an 'affair' baby. I couldn't help but feel curious about whether I had any half-brothers or sisters and wondered if they looked like me. I had now become pretty much a lone wolf and, apart from a couple of semi-serious boyfriends, I had mostly been on my own. Tommo had been the only consistent person in my life, and we had become almost like brother and sister. On one particularly drunken night, we had shared a kiss, but we both very promptly decided that we didn't have those sorts of feelings for each other and promised to wipe the moment from our minds, never to talk of it again. We had continued to have each other's back and although I knew I drove him crazy at times, he still was there at the end of the phone when I needed him.

Standing proudly in the apartment surveying all my hard work, I heard footsteps coming up the wooden stairs from the shop. It was Nika, and in her hand she held a cup of steaming coffee, which she handed to me.

"This place looks so different," Nika enthused, sipping from her own cup. "It reminds me of a place I stayed in once with my sister, Amara. She lives in Florida with her husband now." It was the first time Nika had mentioned any of her family, and I felt pleased that she had opened up to me, a little.

"Is Amara your younger or older sister?" I asked, not sure if she would once again clam up or change the subject.

"She is my twin," Nika smiled, her face lighting up proud. "I don't see her much now, but we talk on the phone a lot."

"You are a twin? Wow, Nika, I had no idea. That's wonderful," I beamed. "Are you identical twins?"

"No, we aren't identical, but we do look very alike. She is far more sensible than me too; I was always the slightly wild one growing up," She laughed.

"Oh, great! Now you tell me," I laughed.

"I promise I will behave and work hard for you, boss," Nika replied, giving me a salute and giggling.

I was still intrigued by her story, and I felt like there was so much more to her than met the eye, but I would let her tell me in her own time. For now, I was grateful to have found someone who slotted into the job role so easily and I wasn't about to rock the boat.

Chapter Eleven

I am sure most people are familiar with the term 'honey-trapping'? If you aren't, I will quickly explain. Honey-trapping is a way of testing a boyfriend/fiancé/husband's loyalty, by placing them in a situation of temptation. Of course, this can also be done to anyone, male or female, but for now, I decided to only offer my services to suspicious wives and girlfriends.

Honey-trapping was one of the services I was offering, via my 'Black Blooms' website and apart from the disastrous 'Jay' job, which wasn't strictly a honey trap, but more of a spying job, I hadn't done anything like it before. Well, that was until now.

The job that came through was a true honey-trap job and I was asked to tempt a woman's husband, who was suspected of cheating with many women. He sounded like an easy target and as usual I did my background work, which was easier this time as both the wife, Keira, and her husband, were very active on social media. They certainly seemed like the perfect couple and had only been married three years.

I always find it amazing and, to be honest, fairly scary how social media can make people's lives look so perfect on the outside, when behind it all is a cesspool of lies, infidelity and heartbreak. But, without all that, I suppose people like me wouldn't have the chance to earn money righting these wrongs or at least exposing them. It's a dirty job but someone has to do it.

The concerned wife, or doormat, as I referred to these people, who allowed their spouses to treat them like crap, had kept me informed of any boy's nights out her husband, Bronson, was having. So, I was ready to go as soon as I got word he was heading out again. When the message came through, we had agreed on a price of $200 with yours truly providing evidence of her husband's reaction on video tape. I always insist on the money being transferred before I head out on a job, for obvious reasons, and everything was going as it was supposed to.

I had decided to go as a redhead on this particular job and with a red off-the-shoulder top, tight leather leggings and a pair of killer red heels. I felt I had really nailed the 'Jessica Rabbit' look. Arriving at my destination, a well-known place called the 'Blue Tiger', I made my way to the bar to order a drink and made myself comfortable on a high, leather-padded stool. The bar was already quite busy so, ordering a Margarita, I subtly scanned the growing crowd for my target. From the photos on social media, he looked to be a pretty tall guy so I was hoping he would literally stand out from the crowd.

It turned out that Saturday night is band night and tonight, it was the turn of 'The Smoke Teasers', who apparently, according to the barman, were one of the most popular bands in L.A. I had never personally heard of them but, judging by how packed the place was getting, I guess they were well known. The growing mass of bodies was going to prove tricky for me to find Bronson, so it was time to think on my feet. Leaving my jacket on the bar stool I headed to the ladies' toilets and hovered by the door. Pulling out my cell, I dialled the bar's number and when one of the barmen picked up, I asked him to do a shout out for Bronson, convincing him that it was a medical emergency.

The barman obliged gladly, and I could soon hear him shouting "Is there a Bronson here?" until he got a response from the crowd. I watched from my vantage point as a tall guy made his way through the excited crowd and took the phone from the waiting barman.

"Hello, this is Bronson," Bronson called into the receiver.

Putting on my best fake squeaky voice, I replied, "Is that Mr James Bronson?"

"No, this is Bronson Prince." The guy replied curtly.

"I am so sorry, wrong person," I squeaked and hung up.

Diving back to the bar, I watched as a confused Bronson chatted to the barman, who just shrugged and hung up the phone. As he went to turn to walk away, I subtly stepped into his path causing him to knock me with his shoulder, resulting in me spilling my drink down my front.

"Oh God, I'm so sorry, I didn't see you," Bronson quickly apologised, handing me some serviettes from the bar to clean up my top.

"No, it was my fault. I wasn't looking," I replied, taking the tissues and dabbing my ample chest with them.

As I looked up and made eye contact with him, my heart skipped a few beats. This guy was seriously good looking, with deep blue eyes and perfect jawline. I literally had to snap my own jaw shut before I started drooling. I had obviously seen what he looked like from his social media posts, but he was so much better looking in the flesh. No wonder he was a supposed woman magnet, with that face. "Concentrate Velvet!", I admonished myself.

"Please, let me get you another drink," Bronson insisted. I just nodded and blinked.

I really, really needed to pull myself together and be professional about this, and quickly.

Popping myself back onto the barstool, I made small talk with Bronson as he ordered and paid for another Margarita and a bottle of Corona for himself. Scanning his hands, I realised he wasn't wearing a wedding ring and from the flirty behaviour I was receiving from him, it was crystal clear, that this guy was indeed a serial cheat. In my handbag, positioned just so, was my burner cell and I had already set it recording, ready to capture whatever was about to happen.

"Are you meeting up with anyone tonight? I've not seen you in here before?" Bronson smiled as he leaned in closer to hear my reply over the noise of the packed bar.

"I'm new in town and I've come to meet up with a girlfriend of mine who said the bands here are pretty cool," I replied, quickly acting like I was new in town. "But she has just texted to say she is running late."

"What a shame! I will just have to keep you company until she arrives then, won't I?" Bronson winked, taking a swig of his drink.

"That's so kind of you, but don't you have a girlfriend or friends waiting for you? I asked, curious as to what his answer would be.

"The boys I'm with are over there having a laugh and they won't miss me for a little bit. I'm single sadly, but I'm hoping to remedy that soon," he grinned.

With a loud cheer, 'The Smoke Teasers' started their set and talking to Bronson became virtually impossible over the deep throbbing base.

"Let's continue this outside," Bronson yelled in my ear and grabbing my hand he guided me through the crowd to the back smoking area, which was now fairly deserted.

"So, what's this friend of yours called?" Bronson asked as I pulled my denim jacket on to fend off the cool evening air.

"She's called Donna," I smiled. "I'm sure she will be along real soon but I'm glad you're keeping me company."

With my heart beating faster by the second, I froze as Bronson reached out and tucked my hair behind my ear. I suddenly started to panic that he would realise I was wearing a wig so reaching up, I took his hand, guiding it back down to my hip.

"I think I might need another drink," I giggled, holding up my now empty glass.

"That can wait," Bronson whispered as he pressed his body against mine, backing me up against the rough brickwork of the wall behind me.

Something had changed in his eyes and a bit of panic and anger started to rise up inside me.

"Okay, stop. I'm not that kind of girl." I spat angrily, pushing him back firmly and realising it was time to get out of there, I tried to get past him.

"I know exactly what you are, you little bitch." he growled, grabbing my throat with his left hand and slamming me back against the wall. "My wife put you up to this, didn't she? Another talentless bimbo who thinks she can trick me into a quick divorce."

The force of my head hitting the rock-hard brick work made me dizzy and disorientated for a few seconds. Then, feeling his hand go across my mouth to stop me screaming, I really started to panic. I realised quickly that we were out of sight of anyone else and with the music blaring out, no one would hear me scream, even if I could. But then, something inside me stirred and my inner fight and rage broke free.

As he tried to force his hands between my legs, I bought my knee up and, with all the strength I had, I smashed him straight in the groin. The force of my blow made him crumple enough for me to dive past him, but unfortunately for me, he recovered and was quick enough to grab my ankle. With a yank, he bought me tumbling down hard on the patio. I was now in real trouble and as he wrenched at my hair, my wig came off. As he forced my head down on the cold, hard stone, he wrapped his huge hands around my throat and began to squeeze. I was powerless. With the last breath I had, I tried to push him off, but he was too big and too strong for my slight frame. Then, just before I felt like I was going to black out, I heard a loud smashing sound and suddenly his weight was lifted. I was free!

    Gasping and scrabbling away, I got shakily to my feet and put my hand to my lip, which was now split and bleeding. Still dazed, I turned around to see a woman standing over the now dazed Bronson, her stiletto heel pressed against his throat and part of a broken chair in her hand. It was Nika.

Chapter Twelve

I didn't remember much of what happened in the few minutes after getting up from the ground. It was all still a bit of a blur, but I do remember Nika, pulling the car over a little up the highway and asking me if I was okay.

"I don't know, I think so," I murmured, still in complete shock at what had just happened at 'The Blue Tiger'.

"Velvet, you were so lucky I was there, because if I hadn't been, God knows what would have happened to you," Nika replied, her voice slightly scolding. "Who was that pig? A date? An ex-boyfriend?"

"He was just some guy," I lied. I didn't want to get into all the gritty details of what I was really doing at the bar. I just wanted to get home.

"Don't lie to me Velvet," Nika chided. "I know exactly why you were there, but I thought I would give you the chance to tell me the truth." Her eyes were fixed on me now and I could now see there was something she wasn't telling me.

"You know that guy, don't you? You know who Bronson is?" I gasped, wincing as pain shot through my smashed lip and bruised head.

"Let's get you fixed up and then we can chat. I will tell you everything if you tell me everything, okay?" Nika was talking calmly but firmly now and I just nodded in agreement.

Nika drove a short distance to a nearby 24-hour drug store and went in to get antiseptic wipes and band aids. While she was gone, I examined my battered face in the visor mirror and for the first time in quite a long time, I felt very vulnerable. Along with my split lip and the growing egg-shaped lump on my forehead, I could feel that the back of my head was sticky with blood. I also realised that one of my earrings had been ripped out and my throat was sore from Bronson's attack.

When Nika returned to the car, she handed me a cup of strong coffee and a chocolate bar. "Get these down you," she smiled. "The sugar and caffeine will make you feel much better."

"Thank you." I whispered, my voice breaking slightly with emotion. Taking a sip of the hot coffee and a careful bite of the chocolate bar, I did instantly feel better.

After Nika had gently cleaned and dressed my wounds, we sat in silence for a few moments, as if neither one of us wanted to start the conversation about Bronson and tonight's events.

"So, how do you know that guy?" I asked Nika, my self-pity was now starting to turn into anger, and I wanted to know everything about this thug.

"You first," Nika replied. "Although I am pretty sure I know you were there to set him up?"

How the hell did Nika know what I was doing there? Had she followed me?

With a deep breath, I proceeded to tell her everything about what I was doing there and how it was my first proper honey-trap job. Nika listened carefully, not saying a word until I had finished. Taking my hand in hers she squeezed it hard.

"That man is well known for his infidelities and violent temper. His wife has been trying to divorce him for months now and she has tried to set him up on numerous occasions, without success. Bronson is too clever, and he can sniff out a honey-trap from a mile away," Nika explained, as I sat open-mouthed listening.

"How do you know all this?" I asked her, already guessing how she knew the whole story.

"I don't think you need to be an expert to work out what sort of work I used to be in, but I will tell you anyway," Nika smirked. "I was an escort turned honey-trapper for a couple of years before I decided the job wasn't for me. It was great money, but there are a lot of guys out there to be wary of and Bronson is one of the worst I've met."

"Who did you work for?" I asked, curious to know more and also a little shocked at what Nika was telling me.

"I signed up with a proper escort agency at first, it was all totally above board and I spent most of my jobs being treated to expensive meals and nights out at the casino. But then, one of the girls in the agency told me about her honey-trapping side-line. I thought it sounded quite cool, so I gave it a go, but it wasn't for me," she explained.

"So, was Bronson one of the jobs you had?" I gasped, worried that Nika had been through what I had just been through.

"No, not me, another girl. She wasn't the brightest, bless her heart, and Bronson soon cottoned on to what she was doing. After she got into his car, he assaulted her very badly and I mean *very* badly." Nika croaked, her voice crumbling as she relayed the story.

"Was she okay?" I asked carefully, terrified of what the answer would be.

"She survived, but only just! He dumped her out on the highway a few miles away, she was found by an elderly couple and taken to hospital. I went and saw her a few times to make sure she was alright, but then, when she was well enough, she just took off to another state and I never heard from her again." Nika shrugged, shaking her head as she remembered it all.

"Oh, my God. Why has this guy not been arrested?" I cried. "Surely the cops would have done him for that?"

"There were no witnesses, and the cops don't have much pity for girls doing that sort of work." Nika gave a sympathetic smile. "For the last few months, I have been following that pig and working out how I could make him pay for what he did to Monica, then you showed up tonight. Of course, I didn't know it was you at first, until he wrenched that wig off your head, but it didn't matter who it was, I still would have smashed the chair over his head."

"I can't imagine what would have happened to me if you hadn't done that." I gasped, grabbing Nika in a tight hug. "Thank you is not good enough."

Finishing the last of my coffee and chocolate we sat silently in Nika's car, both of us probably thinking the same thing.

After pulling out my burner cell from my jacket pocket, I switched it on. The screen had a long crack running across it as a result of me hitting the rock-hard patio, but thankfully it was working fine. The video clearly showed our interaction at the bar and everything else, up to when I hit the patio, but a lot of what went on outside and my assault was just sound. Bronson's body had blocked the camera and there was no clear evidence of what he had done. Despite the lack of video images, the sound of my muffled, terrified voice sent ice cold chills down my spine. I had been so lucky to have got away with a few bumps and scrapes, I owed my life to Nika.

"So what are we going to do about this guy?" I asked Nika straight. This was a shared vengeance now and it had to be clever.

Nika looked at me deeply with her big, beautiful eyes, wearing a devilish grin and simply replied. "Revenge, a whole lot of badass revenge!"

Holding out my now less shaky hand to her, I smiled, "Count me in."

***

When I finally got back to the apartment, I went straight to the bathroom and peered at my battered face in mirror. My eyes worked their way down to the reddening hand mark that had appeared on my throat. The self-pity and shock I had been feeling was now changing into a red-hot anger, not just anger at the animal that had done this, but anger at his wife who, without any warning whatsoever, had sent me into that situation knowing full well what had happened to a previous girl.

Taking out my cell I sent her a message, letting my fury flow out as I explained in no uncertain terms that she had risked my life for a divorce. I had already received the money from her, but it was a pittance for what she had put me through.

A message pinged almost straight back, a heartfelt, grovelling apology, begging for forgiveness and that she had only done it out of pure desperation. She went on to tell me that she was completely trapped by Bronson and had no way of escape as the house and most of their assets were in his name. The only way to get an equal half was if he was found to have committed a felony, or cheated during their marriage, as stated in the pre-nup agreement they had both signed.

This all sounded plausible enough, but why not just walk away from this, moneyless but alive? I sure would. I messaged her back saying as much and her reply was simple. She wanted revenge for what he had done to her, and she was not going to back down and let him get away with everything. She wanted to fight for what was rightfully hers and make sure that no other woman was put in her situation. She had called the cops on him a number of times, but he was so good at covering his tracks and could talk a good game, convincing the officers that she had inflicted the injuries herself and had mental health issues.

Bronson it seemed, had even shown the officers his wife's medical notes, stating that she suffered with anxiety and paranoia. She confirmed this was true many years ago but for the cops, it was enough to walk away. As a final twist of the knife, Bronson had told her that he would kill her should she call the cops again.

I suddenly felt a huge amount of sympathy for this woman and, despite risking another woman's life, I knew she had only done it as she was totally frantic for help. I replied, one final time to her saying that I hoped she stayed safe. Bronson would be going back into that house and who knows what he would do to her after she tried to set him up again. Her reply came back simply saying, "Tonight he just laughed at me! That hurts more than the beatings."

This guy was going to get what was coming to him and I was going to make sure that he paid for what he had done. Karma was coming for him, and it was coming like a steam train.

Chapter Thirteen

It had taken me a few days to recover from what Bronson had done. My lip was still bloodied and fat and the hand marks on my throat had turned into a brownish sort of bruise. Nika had taken over the running of' Lily's' and had told anyone asking where I was that I had a virus and was recovering in bed. The only illness I really had was the self-conscious one that ate away inside me, telling me I was stupid to put myself in that much danger, that I should have researched this guy more thoroughly. I honestly thought putting on a nice dress and a wig, to go flirt with some woman's husband, would be an easy earner. How wrong I was!

Whilst I was hiding away up in the apartment, I had some time to seriously think about where I next went with the 'Black Blooms' website. Should I shut it down? Should I get Nika on board and have her as my official wing woman? Just then, there was a tap at the door and in walked Tommo.

"Jesus, look at you." He winced as he placed a bottle of red wine and a box of pastries on my kitchen counter. "Mr Lin said these were your favourites. Not sure you can enjoy them though with a lip that size."

"I'll force them down." I grinned. "Thanks for coming over to see me."

"Well, I guessed from your text that something pretty bad had happened, so I thought I best stick my head in and check on you." Tommo winked, shoving a whole pastry into his mouth, and then dived onto my couch, patting the cushion beside him in, an invitation to join him.

"I will tell you everything, but you have to promise that you won't lecture me," I told him as I slumped down on the couch beside him. Unwinding the scarf that was around my neck and revealing the bruised handprint on my throat, I watched as his face dropped.

"Christ, who the hell did that, Velvet?" Tommo gasped. "They need a meeting with me and a baseball bat, down a dark alley."

"You don't need to meet anyone anywhere," I told him straight, my tone calm and strong. "We have it in hand. That's all you need to know."

"We? Who is we?" he asked, his eyes not blinking.

"Nika and I. She was the one that put the chair across this guy's head when he was on top of me, smashing my head onto the concrete and trying to strangle me," I explained, a lump catching in my throat as I re-lived what had happened.

"How long have you two been working together doing this?" Tommo questioned.

"Nika works for me in the store, I was out on my own at this bar doing a job when it all went very wrong and it was just by luck that she was there," I replied. "Like I said, I will tell you the full story of what has gone on, but you have to promise to sit and listen."

"Fine," Tommo tutted, holding his hands up as if to surrender. "But you'd best make me a cup of coffee first."

An hour or so later, Tommo had sat and listened to the whole story with very little interruption. I could see from his darkening face, rage was starting to bubble inside him and I was hoping he wouldn't storm off, trying to sort this guy out himself. Any revenge that was owed to Bronson, was owed to me and Nika.

"So, what exactly have you girls got planned for this guy?" Tommo asked, rubbing his stubbled face with his hands.

"We haven't planned anything yet, but whatever we do, will be planned down to the last detail, trust me," I answered. "This guy needs stopping from ever laying a finger on any woman again."

"I agree with that wholeheartedly, Velvet, but you were lucky to get away with your life last time. Is it really worth the risk again? You might not make it back safe this time," he tutted, grumpily.

Tommo was right, of course, and I, of course, knew how lucky I was, but there was something inside me now, burning away, and wanting to be set free. Bronson was going to get what he deserved, that was for sure. We just had to figure out how.

By the time Tommo left, I had been persuaded to allow him in on whatever plan we came up with. I must admit it was a relief to have him on our team, especially with his contacts. I would speak to Nika later and perhaps when I was back up to public appearances, we could get together for a drink. I was sure Tommo and Nika would get along straight away and if they didn't, it was tough. The main problem now was working out exactly what we were going to do to give Bronson the payback he deserved. It was time to get my thinking hat on.

Bronson was clearly a clever guy and would now be even more on guard than he was before. Stalking his Facebook page, I came across a photo of him and Keira. It was taken a day ago and from the looks of Keira's blank, dark eyes, and fake smile, we had to do something soon. Looking at Bronson's smug, grinning face gave me chills and I had a flashback of having his hand around my throat. I could easily just walk away from all of this, but I knew Nika wouldn't, and I owed her big time. Plus, I wanted my own vengeance and I wanted him to be the victim for once.

I needed to put in some proper groundwork first and, making myself comfortable on the couch again, I started to stalk Bronson properly. It was easy enough to find out that he owned a car sales business called 'Princeton Motors', a few miles away from the 'Blue Tiger' bar, that specialised in pimped up, over-priced rides. The glossy look to the website gave it an upmarket, cool look, but I imagined, if the business was anything like Bronson, there was a dark side to it beneath. I needed to find what the darkness was because this was where I imagined it would be best to hit Bronson: in the wallet.

From what I had dug up online the business was solely in Bronson's name and therefore anything we did to bring his business and Bronson to their knees wouldn't affect his wife Keira's pay out, if and when, she did get one. Sending a quick screen shot of the 'Princeton Motors' website over to Tommo, to see if he knew of it, I headed into the bathroom. After applying some concealer to what was left of my bruises on my face and wrapping a light scarf around my neck, I headed downstairs to see how Nika was doing in the shop.

"Feeling better then?" Nika beamed as she saw me. Her smile was enough to light up anyone's mood and I instantly felt restored.

"Oh yes, thank you. I am feeling much better and ready for action," I smiled back. "I can't thank you enough for what you have done for me in the last few days, and I will make sure you get a decent bonus in your paycheck this week, I promise."

"It's not necessary, really," Nika began to argue. "I would have done that for anyone, especially a friend and that is exactly what you are."

"You can say what you like, you are getting a bonus," I replied firmly and Nika rolled her eyes at me, then turned her attention to a customer who walked in holding one of the pre-tied bouquets that Nika had placed out the front of the store. The bouquet was stunning, a real rainbow of colour, tied together with raffia and Nika had cleverly used a lot of the less popular flowers which, when used together, were irresistible to anyone walking by.

"Those are beautiful," I whispered to her as she handed over the customer's change and bid them goodbye.

"I just thought they made a good combination and thought I would try some ready tied bouquets outside, to see if they sold. I hope you don't mind?" Nika replied, screwing her face up slightly in uncertainty.

"How many have you sold?" I asked her.

"I made ten bunches up from the slower selling flowers and I think that was the last bunch." Nika beamed.

"I most certainly don't mind, and I am delighted you used your initiative to turn something unpopular into a star-selling item," I laughed. "Please don't ever worry about trying new ideas. I totally trust you to make decisions like that."

Nika blushed and smiled as she looked down at her feet. I didn't think anyone had ever really praised her before and she almost looked emotional.

"How about we lock up early tonight and I treat you to a take-out? It's the least I can do," I suggested.

"That sounds amazing. Yes, please if you are sure?" Nika nodded.

"Excellent! We can turn it into a bit of a business meeting too, as I've got some things to show you on what I've found out about this Bronson guy," I suggested.

Later that evening, as we tucked into Pad Thai and peanut chicken, from my favourite restaurant round the corner, I showed Nika the 'Princeton Motors' website and the messages I had received from his wife, Keira. She agreed that, somehow taking down his business was a better and safer plan, but she also made it clear that Bronson also needed to have a taste of his own medicine.

"Do you mean physically hurt him?" I asked, a bit shocked.

"He deserves everything he gets," Nika growled, as she downed a glass of red wine.

"You already hit him with a chair." I laughed, trying to break the tension. "You could have been done for assault had we not got out of there so quick."

"And he could have killed you if I hadn't," Nika said coldly. "It was self-defence. Who knows what else this guy has done to other women?"

She was right, of course, and there was a part of me that really, really wanted to make him pay for what he had put myself, Nika's friend and Keira through, but this guy was not going to be an easy target. We had to be clever, keep ourselves out of danger and out of jail.

Hearing my cell ping, I picked it up and saw that Tommo had replied to my earlier message. He suggested that we meet up at the bar in a couple of days' time, after he had done some digging on Bronson's car business. Nika nodded in agreement. It was clear that she wanted revenge on Bronson sooner rather than later. I was hoping that she wouldn't go all mercenary on me and take matters into her own hands. She, of all people, knew how dangerous this guy was and who else he was mixed up with.

After a couple of glasses of wine, I made Nika make me a promise she would not do her own, lone wolf, revenge thing and I could only trust her when she said she wouldn't. Hopefully, Tommo would be able to give us some useful information and together we could make a plan that we could all agree on. Everyone had a weakness and there would be some way we could find the chink in Bronson's armour. We just had to find it. I had a feeling there was something Nika was not telling me, something she was holding back about Bronson. Did she know something we didn't? Her need for revenge was so red-hot, it burned in her eyes whenever the subject was bought up and it uneased me a little.

I guessed I would figure that out soon, too. Nika was really still a stranger and in a lot of ways a closed book, which I understood because, after all, that was what I was to her. Trust had to be earned and so far, we were starting to trust each other, and both had opened up a little about our pasts. If I wanted to find out what was really under her skin, I would have to do it carefully and even perhaps without her knowing.

Chapter Fourteen

A couple of days later, with my face more or less healed and carefully applied make-up covering what bruising I had left, Nika and I headed down to the bar to meet with Tommo. I was keen to know what Tommo had found out about Bronson's business and hoped that he had found us some decent dirt to go on.

The bar was, as usual, pretty busy with its typical grungy crowd and as we walked through towards the back where Tommo was sat in his usual booth, I watched as people's eyes followed Nika as she glided through the tables. She was a stranger in this place and that, coupled with her exotic beauty, was sure to turn heads. I did wonder if anyone recognised her, even though she had told me she wasn't from round here.

Tommo got to his feet as we reached his booth and after giving him a quick kiss and hug, I introduced him to Nika, who held out her slender hand for him to shake, before taking a seat next to me at the table. I could tell

Nika was slightly anxious about being in a place she didn't know and decided that alcohol was the ideal icebreaker. I offered to go and get us a round of drinks and headed to the bar, leaving Tommo and Nika getting to know each other.

Ordering our usual beers, plus some Old Fashioneds, I headed back with a laden tray to see how the conversation was going. There seemed to be some sort of joke going on and as I carefully placed the drinks on the table, Tommo looked up and grinned at me.

"What?" I asked, giving him a sideways look. "What's so funny?"

"I was just saying to Nika how we should congratulate you for managing to buy a round of drinks without kicking anyone in the balls today," he cackled, giving me one of his usual, cheeky winks.

"Ha, bloody ha!" I sighed, trying not to smile. "I only defend myself when I have to and this time there were no creepy guys trying to hit on me at the bar, so it's all good."

"That's because they are all too afraid to approach you now, you know." Tommo grinned, covering his privates with his hands mockingly.

"You think you are so bloody funny, don't you?" I laughed, rolling my eyes as I sat down next to Nika again. "So come on then, let's get down to business. What have you found out about the car place?"

"Well, I did do some digging like I was asked and all I can say is, this Bronson bloke is tied up with some pretty dodgy guys," Tommo replied, folding his arms across his chest as he leaned back against the booth seat.

"Do you mean dodgy, as in risky for him, or risky for us?" I asked, concerned that it might be too dangerous to go after this guy after all.

"Let's just say that Bronson is up to his neck in debt with his car business and he had to take out some serious credit with some, less than friendly, Chinatown gangsters," Tommo continued.

From what I knew about the Chinatown gangsters, it wasn't the best situation for Bronson to be in and it was no wonder he was less than keen for his wife to divorce him taking half his money. No wonder he resorted to threats and violence to try and protect what little he did actually own, or half-own.

"How deep is this guy in debt with these Chinatown people?" Nika asked suddenly, her voice calm and cold. "Is he likely to get bumped off before we can do anything to him?"

Tommo shook his head. "No, I doubt it. It appears that our friend, Bronson, is having to allow the good Chinatown folk to use his motor sales business, not only to distribute a healthy supply of top-class cocaine, but also to help wash some of the proceeds from it."

"Jesus!" I breathed, shifting in my seat uncomfortably. "This guy has much bigger problems than us coming after him then?"

"You could say that, yes." Tommo replied.

"So, what do we do now?" Nika asked, her eyes firmly fixed on the beer mat she was shredding into tiny pieces. "I want that guy to pay for what he has done, and I don't want to sit back while others take our chance of getting it."

Tommo and I exchanged a look between us, and I gave him a nod.

"Look, Nika, this may not be as straightforward as we first thought. We could end up in a pretty deadly situation if we get too close to this car place, especially if it is being used to traffic drugs and wash money. It sounds to me like this guy's days are numbered anyway," I said, calmly.

"You two can do what you like, but this guy needs to pay for what he did to my friend and for what he did to you, Velvet. Don't you want to help bring this guy to his knees?" Nika snapped, slamming her fist on to the table and bringing a brief hush to the whole bar.

Grabbing Nika's wrist before she could slam her fist down again, I looked her straight in the eye. "Nika, I never said we weren't going after this guy. I just said it wouldn't be that straightforward. I can see how much this means to you and trust me, I want my own retribution, but we have to go about this with extreme caution."

I could see Nika's amber-tinged eyes were now brimmed with tears, I imagined with either frustration or anger, probably both. It was obvious this meant a lot more to her than I had first thought, it made me sick to my stomach to imagine what injuries Bronson had inflicted on her friend Monica to promote this sort of reaction.

Despite my usual 'act first, think later' attitude, I now found myself in a calm, but decisive, state of mind and wrapping an arm around Nika's shoulders, I pulled her into me, allowing her to sob briefly and to allow any anger to ebb away.

"I swear to you that we will make this guy pay for what he did to me and Monica, but first we need to do a bit more digging and find out what we can about how Bronson runs the car business, before any of us does anything. Deal?" I said firmly, giving her a last squeeze before releasing her to sit up and finish her drink.

"Deal," Nika nodded, holding out both her hands for Tommo and I to all shake together.

We talked for another two hours at the bar. I kept the drinks flowing while Nika and Tommo scoured the internet for anything useful about 'Princeton Motors'. We needed everything from opening hours to partnerships, if there were any. I wanted to know every detail of how that place ran.

"You two up for a night-time stake out?" I grinned, knowing that Tommo would love to be out playing detective.

"Only if I can bring my binoculars and you buy me a bucket of fried chicken," Tommo beamed.

"Of course there will be fried chicken!" I laughed. "Nika?"

"Count me in too," Nika smiled, raising her glass and clinking it with mine. "I promise I won't go all mercenary on you."

"What a relief," I laughed. "So, is everyone free tomorrow night?"

Tommo and Nika both nodded and we agreed to meet at 10pm at the shop and take two separate vehicles to go and stake out 'Princeton Motors'. Tommo seemed to think that would be a good starting time as the highways would be fairly quiet by then, plus it wasn't too early for dodgy dealings to take place. We could, of course, sit there for hours for absolutely nothing to happen, but Tommo was confident that something was happening most nights. He wouldn't reveal his sources, but I guessed it was someone either involved directly with 'Princeton Motors' or the Chinatown gangsters. I was more than happy not to know.

Checking on my burner phone, which had been vibrating away in my jacket pocket off and on throughout the evening, I found a new message from the 'Black Blooms' website. I hadn't done any extra work since the attack at the 'Blue Tiger' and the thought of it happening again was still very much on my mind. This order was for 'Pink Peonies', sounded a bigger job than the last and would therefore cost more.

"Another job?" Tommo asked, nodding towards my cell as I placed it on the table.

I nodded and took a large gulp of my beer. "It can wait," I shrugged, trying to act nonchalantly about it, but I could feel Tommo's eyes searching my face.

"You could just close it down," he suggested, giving me a small reassuring smile.
He was right, of course. I had the power to just shut down the whole thing with the click of a button, but I wasn't ready to do that yet. The money was good from these sorts of jobs and I still got a kick out of helping people realise the vengeance they deserved.

"It's only a little job and it sounds like fun." I winked. "It might even be a job where I require a wingman or woman."

Nika immediately sat up tall and gave me a quick mock salute. "I am here ready and waiting, Captain Darke," she laughed.

"Excellent! I need a deputy." I nodded.

Dropping Nika off outside her small dark apartment block, I watched as she swayed her way up the concrete steps and paused at the top to wave me goodbye. She was going to make a perfect wing-woman for my next job, which from what I could tell from the message, involved more than was listed on the 'Black Blooms' website. It was definitely a job for two of us. In brief, the client was asking for vengeance on her manager who, after five years of loyal service, had fired her without warning, to take on a younger, prettier girl. The message read like a story from a soap drama. It would have been a simple job of petty revenge on his company car or business, had it not been for the fact that the manager had apparently framed this poor cashier with theft. The store in question was part of a well-known clothing chain, in which I myself had shopped there regularly.

I, of course, asked for evidence of the wrongful firing. Within an hour, my inbox filled with photos of the "stolen" item, a crystal encrusted necklace, and a photo taken from security footage, allegedly showing the manager hiding the necklace in his office. After squinting at the photo, it did look like he was carrying a necklace, but the image was blurry and it was hard to tell.

I had messaged back saying that I needed to see more evidence before taking any job on and almost immediately a message pinged back simply saying:

"*Petra said you could help me.*"

That was all I needed to convince myself this job was indeed genuine. I sent a message back asking exactly what sort of revenge she was after and how far she wanted me to take it. The client's reply was again fast and simple:

"I am happy to pay $200 to watch him squirm. I will leave the rest up to you."

This was sounding like quite a fun job, so the next morning, after Nika and I had opened up the shop, I told her all about it. As I was telling her about what I was planning, her eyes glinted with excitement, and she started to laugh loudly.

"Okay, what's so funny?" I asked, feeling a bit puzzled by her reaction.

Nika hopped up on to the counter and still laughing to herself, she told me that she had gone to that very store to apply for a job interview. After waiting in the manager's office for ten minutes, he had marched in, taken one look at her and told her that the position had already been filled.

"I knew exactly why he had said it," Nika said, a flash of anger crossing her face as she remembered what had happened. "As I had walked through the store, I realised that every member of staff was young, pretty and white! I refused to leave the office until he told me the real reason for not giving me an interview and after a brief argument, he simply stated that "I didn't have the right image for the store".

"That is beyond disgusting," I sighed, shaking my head in disbelief. "This guy sounds like a real piece of work and it's about time he was bought back down to earth."

"I literally can't wait." Nika beamed, rubbing her hands together in anticipation.

We spent most of the morning discussing how, and when, we could take on this job, all the while, trying to quell Nika's growing excitement as she planned more and more elaborate and, quite frankly, alarming ways of getting revenge. I had been quite firm and insisted we stick to whatever plan we agreed on to the letter, especially being my first job back after being attacked. Nika had crossed her heart and promised that she would go along with any plan I came up with, to the letter. I had no choice but to trust her and I must admit I was really looking forward to doing this job with her by my side.

My plan was a simple one. We were to go to the clothing store, just before closing and hide amongst the clothing until the place was closed and empty. I then planned to creep to the office, while Nika kept a look out, and search the place until I found the missing necklace. I would then place the necklace somewhere where another staff member would find it and we would leave.

I had spent a while discussing the security setup with my client, she had quite happily told me where the blind spots on the CCTV were and the alarm code for the building. What she couldn't' guarantee was that the delightful manager hadn't changed the code. She said it was doubtful because he wasn't the brightest and would be too lazy to ring the alarm company to organise changing it.

With the plan now formed we agreed to pay the store a visit that night, just in case the necklace got moved, and our efforts were for nothing. Nika was now known to the store manager, so we altered the plan slightly, so that I would go in and hide in the store until it was locked up and quiet, then I would disable the alarm and let Nika in through the back entrance.

"What do I wear tonight?" Nika asked keenly, as she helped me bring in the last of the flowers from the display outside.

"I would wear simple, dark clothing. And tuck your hair up into a hat?" I suggested. "That's what I am going to wear, plus of course, comfortable footwear in case any running is required," I winked.

"This is going to be so much fun!" Nika giggled, pulling on her dark denim jacket. "I will be ready to go at 6pm as planned?"

"I will be waiting outside for you." I nodded, and after waving her off down the street, I locked the door behind her and raced up stairs to get ready. It was already 5pm and I wanted to have a play with a few new looks I had been working on, ready for any upcoming jobs.

Opening my wardrobe wide I felt a little tingle inside. I still felt like a little girl, raiding her mother's closet, to play dress up except, all of this was mine and I was going to be playing dress up for real. Opting for a mahogany brown, bob-cut look tonight, I coupled it with a dark navy, turtleneck, which I tucked into a pair of black high-waisted jeans. With a sprinkle of jewellery and a pair of sneakers, I was ready to roll. It wasn't my most glamorous look, but it was effective enough to give me a demure 'I'm just out shopping 'look, which would hopefully not draw too much attention.

Taking a quick selfie, I sent the photo over to Nika, who quickly sent one back of herself. She was wearing a black long-sleeved top and black leather look trousers and looked like she could have stepped on to a film set.

"Looking hot, but don't forget a hat!" I sent back, with a smiley face emoji.

I was starting to feel the start of nerves forming deep in my stomach now, just like I always did before heading out. But taking one last look in the mirror, I grabbed my keys and headed off to pick up Nika.

Chapter Fifteen

"Ready to go shopping?" Nika grinned as she sprang into the passenger seat of Mr Lin's little car. She was wearing a beanie-type hat with her hair tucked up inside, but still somehow looked like she was off to a fashion shoot.

"I'm ready if you are?" I laughed, her chilled out vibe relaxing me slightly.

As we headed across town, the sun was starting to set, casting an amber coloured glow to highlight everything it touched as it lowered behind the tall buildings lining the freeway.

Pulling up in the parking lot beside Morgan's fashion store, we surveyed the surroundings. We agreed to park a little way out of sight of any cameras that would be used by the store to cover the immediate parking spaces. Nika was to wait in the car while I went into the store and she would watch from a distance as the store was locked up for the evening, hopefully with me hidden inside. We had already planned on it being at least an hour before all of the staff had finished cashing up and left, then I would message her from inside, once the coast was clear.

Grabbing my handbag, I headed across the parking lot and made my way inside the store which, thankfully, was still pretty busy, due to having a sale on. This would work in my favour as the staff probably wouldn't notice if I vanished when they had plenty of other customers to deal with.

Making my way round the store, I acted like a real shopper, taking items down and looking at them held up against me in front of the many mirrors that hung along the whitewashed walls. There were some really pretty dresses that caught my eye, but I had to remind myself, I was there to do a job, not to shop for real. I had counted five members of staff on the store floor, including two young girls working the tills, but was yet to spot my main target, the manager.

From what I had found out about Gavin Grimstone, the balding, slightly overweight manager of Morgan's fashion store; he was a twice divorced father of two and had worked at the store for over nine years. He liked golf, fast cars and, from I could tell from the staff, he also liked to be surrounded by pretty young girls!

After wandering around for twenty minutes, I spotted a tall rack of maxi dresses and after having a quick flick through them, I figured I could easily slip between them and stand with my back against the wall, totally hidden from sight. It was only ten minutes now until closing time and announcements were being called out, alerting shoppers that the store was due to close shortly and asking them to make their way to the cashier's desk with their purchases.

In the centre of the store stood three mannequins, balanced high on white gloss boxes, and dressed in the store's most expensive attire. I figured, that with a bit of a knock, the mannequins might just topple off and cause enough distraction for me to disappear into my planned hiding place. It would only need one to topple off and I made my way around the store for the final time and while everyone else queuing to pay for their items, I pretended to lean on the tallest mannequin to adjust my shoe. It was only bolted to the top of the white box by one foot and with a little discreet twist, I freed it and had to dodge quickly out of the way as it began to topple towards me. Giving it a quick push back with my hand, I scuttled off, hoping no one had seen me.

Diving down the lingerie aisle, I hastily made my way towards the dresses' section and winced as I heard a resounding crash behind me, followed by gasps from the few customers that still remained.

Peering out from behind a rack of dresses, I could see that not one, but all three of the mannequins had toppled over in a domino effect, sending plastic body parts rolling about the store floor. A red faced, balding man, who I recognised immediately as Gavin, the store manager, came storming down towards them, shaking his head, and shouting to members of staff to clear up the mess. With chaos ensuing on the shop floor, I managed to slip myself easily and quietly between the dresses, vanishing completely out of sight. Now I had to play a waiting game.

With my heart rate through the roof and my legs beginning to quiver slightly, I wondered what an earth I had got myself into this time. Standing amongst the maxi dresses, hardly daring to breathe, I prayed that the store would be locked up and quiet sooner rather than later. I could hear Gavin, the delightful manager, barking instructions to the three young staff members who were struggling to put back together the dismembered mannequins and mount them back on their stands. It was clear that Gavin was pretty disliked by most, if not all, of his employees and I stifled a giggle as I watched them pull faces behind his back.

It took about forty minutes for the store to be fully locked down after registers were cashed up, floors swept and lights off. I gave it another few minutes before I dared creep out from my hiding spot and head for the alarm panel by the main doors. Shakily, punching in the numbers my client had given me, I held my breath until the alarm showed it had been de-activated. Grabbing my cell, I quickly messaged Nika, who probably thought by now I had been arrested, or worse and told her to head round to the back door, where I could let her in.

Heading through the stock room to find the delivery entrance, I awaited Nika's knock on the door to say, "all was clear" and quickly opened it for her to slip through.

"Right, first things first; we need to sort out the CCTV and make sure anything with us on it, is deleted," I instructed Nika. "Let's find this guy's office, as that's where it will be."

Nika nodded and using the lights on our cells we made our way swiftly up the chrome-coloured stairway to the manager's office. The door was, of course, locked but Nika, without so much as a word or blink, pulled a hair pin out from under her hat and had the door open in a flash. I wasn't sure whether to be relieved, or worried about the skill set Nika was now unveiling but seeing as we needed to be in and out as quickly as possible, I just went with it, and never said a word.

Gavin's office was pretty stark and boring, with only a few filing cabinets lining one wall and a few samples of clothing hung on another. The CCTV screens were located on the left hand-side of his huge wooden desk and with a few presses of various buttons, I managed to rewind the recordings to lunchtime, disabling the cameras from recording any more. It should have been fairly easy to search and after a few minutes of drawing a blank on the location of the necklace, the only other place to look was the locked drawer of his desk.

"Did you bring a crowbar?" Nika asked me.

"Do I look like I came armed with a crowbar?" I scoffed, opening my jacket and giving her a twirl.

"Well, how else are we supposed to bust into locked stuff?" she tutted, before putting her hands on her hips and shaking her head.

"You didn't do a bad job with a hair pin earlier," I winked.

Scanning the office for anything with a sharp edge, my eyes fell upon a knife-like letter opener, which stuck out from beneath some folders on the desk.

Clutching it, I bent down and after a few awkward attempts at picking the lock, the draw sprang open.

"Ta dah!" I beamed, feeling rather proud of myself, before opening the drawer fully and rummaging inside.

"I reckon you have done that a few times before," Nika scoffed, looking impressed.

"I'm learning on the job," I replied, feeling very smug.

The drawer only contained some paperwork and an old copy of a well-read pervy magazine which I fished out and dumped in the nearby trash. Remembering the message, I had been sent by my client, I felt around on the top inside of the drawer and my hand soon found a padded envelope, taped to the underside of the desk. Bingo!

Tipping out the contents of the envelope onto the desk, a big grin spread across my face. We had found the necklace! It shimmered and sparkled in the light, and I thought hard about what to do next. The necklace wasn't the only thing in the envelope: bracelets, earrings and rings also spilled out. It was then obvious this guy had set up more than one person and was clearly making a sideline as well, selling what he had taken. We had been instructed to leave it somewhere obvious for everyone to see when they arrived at work the next morning, but the question was where?

While Nika searched the office for ideas, I quickly made my way downstairs and scanned the store for inspiration. One of the mannequins from earlier was still propped up against its plinth and I suddenly had an idea.

Picking up the mannequin, which was heavier than it looked, I headed back towards the stairs that led to the office. That was when I heard Nika scream, followed by a heavy crash on the floor above. Someone else was here.

Dropping the mannequin and racing up the stairs shouting Nika's name, I burst through the office door to find Gavin, the manager, laying spread-eagled on the carpeted floor, clearly out for the count. Nika stood above him, a computer keyboard in her hand and a horrified look on her face.

"What the hell?" I panted, running to check that Gavin was just knocked out and not dead.

"He just appeared from nowhere, he must have come back for something. I just grabbed the nearest thing and whacked him with it," Nika cried, dropping the keyboard onto the floor like it was suddenly red hot.

"Holy crap, what do we do now?" I hissed, trying desperately to think. "Did he see your face, Nika?"

"No, I was behind the door when he walked in and when I realised it wasn't you, I just freaked and belted him one with the keyboard." Nika explained, her voice trembling.

"Okay. Let's just calm things down and try to think clearly." I breathed slowly, an idea suddenly forming in my mind. "We've wiped the CCTV. He didn't see your face and he obviously didn't spot me downstairs. Quick, let's find his cell and see if he called the cops before he came in."

Patting down Gavin's jacket, Nika soon found his cell phone and checked the screen. It was locked so we had no idea if he had called the cops or had just decided to check out the scene himself first.

"Well, I don't hear any sirens, so I am hoping we are alright for now, but let's just do what we came to do and get out of here sharpish," I said, firmly.

On the floor Gavin was starting to stir and moan and it wouldn't be long before he was conscious. Snatching the clothing samples from the wall, I pulled the thin leather belt off a denim dress and tied Gavin's hands firmly behind his back. While he was still semi-conscious, Nika helped me lift him into his office chair, which was quite an effort, as he wasn't the smallest of guys.

Taking off his tie, I used it to fasten his already tied hands to the back of the chair and with a scarf and pair of sportswear leggings, we bound his feet, blindfolded and gagged him. He looked ridiculous and, as he started to become fully conscious, I placed the necklace round his neck and fastened it at the back. Squatting down by his side, I adjusted the scarf tied around his eyes to reveal one of his ears.

"Hi, Gavin. I'm so sorry it came to this, but we had no choice. We have CCTV tapes of you framing your employees and sexually harassing them. If you go to the cops we will release it all to them, not to mention onto social media. Understood?" I purred.

Gavin was shaking and sweating profusely, trying to wrench himself free, until Nika walked calmly up and pressed the letter opener to his throat.

"Do we understand each other?" I growled into his ear and watched as he nodded frantically.

"Good. Now be a good boy and sit there calmly while we go; I wouldn't want you to fall over and bang your head again," I finished, getting up and patting him on the head, making him flinch slightly.

Opening the printer by the side of his computer, I took out a piece of paper and with a marker pen I wrote in huge letters: PERVERT, RACIST, THIEF. I grabbed a quick shot of the scene for my client on my burner phone while Nika checked for any trace linking us to what we had just done. We had thankfully worn latex gloves so as not to leave any fingerprints behind in case Gavin did call the cops. With everything checked and clear we headed off back down the stairs and out through the rear exit.

Gavin would have a long night to sit and think about what he had done, and it would give his staff a good laugh when they arrived for work the next day. Things hadn't quite gone according to plan, but it was too late now to go back and change things.

Sending the photo off to my client with a note explaining our actions that evening, I contemplated what had just happened. I was forever grateful to have had Nika by my side and it was clear she could handle herself in most situations, even if things did go a bit wrong!

We still had the Bronson situation to resolve and the thought of it still twisted my stomach into an anxious knot.

Tonight's events had once again shown me, that even the best-laid plans can take a different path, we needed to plan for the unexpected and always have a way of getting ourselves out of tight situations. I also needed to re-think my pricing strategy because the risk these jobs were now presenting, were not really worth the reward I was charging. I needed to have something that represented the danger and risk element of more hands-on jobs. Something that stood out, caught people's attention, and gave them a clear indication of what it entailed.

Walking to my windowsill, I lent on the frame and looked out onto the street as I thought. I needed to keep with the flower theme to fit in with the 'Black Blooms' website. Red roses would have been fitting but I'd already used that as code for honey-trapping, orchids would be a good one, but I needed something a level or two up, to represent a special order for a special job. Looking down at the crystal cut vase on my windowsill, I got my answer. There, although slightly wilted now, sat three blood tipped roses. It was perfect as they represented the elegance and strength of the normal rose, but also had a tinge of darkness to their petals. If you ordered a bunch of blood tipped roses via the dark website, it would inform you that these were for a very special occasion and the price would reflect that.

I had no doubt that I would get plenty of work, but I would have to be ultra-careful who I got caught up with and who I would be working for. I wasn't an assassin for hire and there were limits to what I would do, or rather what Nika and I would do.

People like Gavin and Bronson deserved what they got and there were, without doubt, people far, far worse than them who needed similar treatment. Revenge was a profitable game if played right and there did seem to be plenty of people out there, willing to pay whatever it took to see wrongs made right.

I had well and truly got the bug now in the 'Vengeance for hire game' and with it being such a huge city, I wouldn't go short of customers. I would never give up 'Lily's', but this extra work would now give me the opportunity to open another shop perhaps. Maybe one day I would have a whole chain of 'Lily's', spreading out across America or may be even the world! There was nothing wrong with dreaming big and although my little side-line business wasn't exactly legit, I wasn't really harming anyone, just righting a few wrongs whilst getting paid for it. There was still one big wrong to be made right and that was in the form of Bronson Prince. Tomorrow night, we were due to stake out his car business and, after tonight's events, I felt like I was back to something resembling my own self. Looking closely at my neck in the hallway mirror, I could still make out faint bruising from where he had choked me. Nika was right, we couldn't let this go.

Chapter Sixteen

As far as stakeouts go, we were pretty much nailing it. Just like I promised, I made a stop off to buy two buckets of the finest fried chicken in town for us to share, along with gallons of Cola. We headed off in separate cars, Tommo in his own beat-up Nissan and Nika and I in Mr Lin's little run-around.

We had agreed to park up in two separate locations so that we covered, more or less, the whole site of 'Princeton Motors' and could see if anyone was approaching front or rear entrances. The main show room was still brightly lit and an illuminated sign above a huge glass window spelt out its name as it shone in the pitch-black night air. From what I could see, there was no one inside and any cars parked in the dedicated parking lot, were displaying 'For Sale' signs, so I speculated the place was empty.

I messaged Tommo to see if he had seen anything from his vantage point and he simply sent back a 'Not yet!' He was adamant his source would be correct and that something happened most nights, around this time.

Nika was stuffing the fried chicken down like she hadn't been fed for a week, while she chatted away about what had happened in the store today. She had taken a large order for funeral flowers, and it would take both of us a good two days to get the order ready in time for the service. I just hoped that tonight wasn't going to be too long a night, as we would need a bright and early start tomorrow if we were to crack on with the order, as well as running the store.

Twenty minutes later, my cell buzzed with a message from Tommo. It simply read 'We're on!' and I knew instantly he meant deliveries were being made or were about to be made into the showroom.

"Should we move the car?" Nika asked, trying her best to wipe off the grease from her fingers onto a paper serviette.

"I think we should, but we still need to stay well out of sight as they are bound to have lookouts," I replied.

Getting on the wrong side of these Chinatown gangsters would be a disaster and tonight was merely an information gathering exercise.

Easing the car very slowly with the lights off, I parked a little nearer to the show room, just close enough to be able to see, through binoculars, two medium-sized vans reverse into place. Next, two dark-haired men began unloading what looked like boxes with images of shampoo bottles on the side.

"That's a lot of shampoo," I pondered, handing the binoculars to Nika so she could see what was happening.

"I bet those boxes don't contain shampoo." Nika half laughed. "I don't see the delightful Bronson at the moment though."

"No, he is probably at home terrorising his poor wife," I tutted, shaking my head.

"I doubt it," Nika replied. "I would think he'd want to oversee all of this, don't you?" Nika questioned. She was right. It made no sense for Bronson not to be here and my guess was that he was already inside.

"There he is," Nika hissed. "There, behind the van on the right, helping to unload."

Stealing the binoculars back off Nika, I soon spotted Bronson Prince, laughing and joking with the other man as they bought box after box out of the vans. That is a ridiculous amount of shampoo I thought.

"Surely, if the cops had any suspicions of this going on, the place would be raided?" I questioned, finding it hard to believe that any activity at this time of night, would evade the attention of a passing cop car.

"If he is involved with the Chinatown gangsters, I would imagine they have quite an influential hold over the cops, don't you?" Nika said, calmly raising her eyebrows.

She was right, of course. If Bronson was indeed involved with a high up drug and money laundering scam, then there was no way anything like tonight could happen, without some influence over local law enforcement?

Watching the vans finally pull away and disappear into darkness, I wondered if it was the right time to get a closer look at what was going on inside 'Princeton Motors'. I needed to see if Bronson was on his own after the drop-offs, as if he was, it would make him an easier target for a spot of revenge.

"I need a closer look. Swap seats with me and then drive me down to the edge of the parking lot," I instructed Nika.

"Are you completely insane?" Nika spat, almost choking on another piece of fried chicken.

"Do I look like I'm joking?" I replied, my tone firm and calm. "I need to see what goes on inside with all that stuff and if that pig has anyone else in there helping him."

Exiting the car, I ran round to Nika's side and gestured for her to jump across to the driver's seat, which she begrudgingly did, with a lot of muttering. She could see it was a waste of time arguing with me about it. Nika dropped me off by the parking lot entrance, I carefully climbed out of the passenger seat and stood under some small trees that lined the entrance. My cell suddenly started to vibrate in my pocket, and I could see by the screen that it was Tommo calling me.

"What the hell are you doing?" Tommo hissed down the line before I could even answer.

"Just having a little check out. Don't worry," I replied curtly and hung up.

I knew Tommo would be having a pink fit in the car; and I know he only had my best interest at heart, but I knew what I was doing. Flipping up the hood on my zip-through jacket and tucking my hair neatly in, I kept to the treeline until I had reached the wall of the building. Peering into the showroom, I made sure it was clear before I headed round to the rear of the building where the vans had been parked, pausing by the corner of the structure.

Scanning the rooftop for security cameras, I spotted at least two covering this particular area, but my theory was that they would be turned off. Bronson wouldn't want any of his dodgy dealings to be caught on his own CCTV, would he? It was a risk I was willing to take and with my face pretty much covered up by my hoodie, I pressed on. I could hear a man's voice as I neared an open door and was fairly sure it was Bronson's. He was talking fast, and it soon became clear that he was on his own, talking into his cell I stood silently, my body pressed hard against the wall, hidden in the shadow from the roof, listening carefully to what was being said. It is never easy to listen to a one-way conversation but whatever Bronson was discussing, was not a cheerful subject.

"Like we discussed, I promised you I would get you what you wanted, but these things take time," I heard Bronson tell the person on the other end of the call.

"Of course, I understand that, and you must admit, so far I have been a man of my word, have I not? Exactly! All I am asking for, is two more weeks, everything I have planned will be in place and we will all be happy." Bronson's voice was calm but forceful and sneaking a look round the wall, I could see he was pacing up and down, rubbing his hand across his forehead.

"Can we just…" Bronson started to speak again, but it was clear the caller had ended the conversation and hung up. "Screw you!" Bronson screeched into the screen and after repeatedly slamming his palm against the wall, threw his cell at the concrete floor, sending it rebounding and sliding in my direction.

The cell landed literally four feet away from the corner of the wall where I stood, pinned to the brickwork, hardly now daring to breathe. Stomping after his phone, Bronson muttered and swore as he bent down to pick it up and, after pausing for few seconds, literally a few feet from me to check if he had broken it, he turned around and returned indoors.

I felt sick and my heart was racing so fast, I feared it would explode in my chest. But I wasn't going anywhere yet. I needed to look inside to see what else was going on in the back storage room and what was inside those shampoo boxes. Gathering my breath, I took another cautious look and with no sign of Bronson now, I slunk along the wall, keeping my skinny frame hidden in the shadow of the overhanging roof.

I could hear Bronson now, moving boxes while muttering to himself. As I sneaked closer to the open door, I could see he was moving boxes from one area to another. I counted that it took him about twenty-one seconds to walk back and forth from one area to the other. I figured that, if I were quick enough, I could grab a bottle out of one of the open boxes and be out again before being spotted.

This was insane, but I wanted to know what was inside the bottles of shampoo because something told me it wasn't for washing cars. I watched Bronson move back and forth a couple more times and then made my move. Tiptoeing in, I reached the first open box and quickly, but carefully, opened the top to reveal the large bottles inside.

Grabbing one as silently as I could, I eased it out and darted stealthily back to the open door.

That was when something else caught my eye: Bronson's cell. It was balanced on top of one of the stacks of boxes and, with only a split second to act, I took my chance and snatched it up. I stuffed it into my jacket pocket, dived out of the door and slipped away into the night.

Reaching the refuge of the highway, I spotted Nika flash the headlights from where she was now parked and aimed for the sanctuary of the car. I leapt into the passenger seat and told Nika to drive while my own cell buzzed out of control in my pocket.

"What, in God's bloody name, do you think you were doing, Velvet?" Tommo hollered, as I reluctantly answered the call.

"I'm okay, Tommo, calm down, alright? Meet us down at Betty's Diner because I really need a strong coffee," I replied curtly and hung up on him, slumping back in the seat as I composed myself.

"Girl, you literally are one ballsy chick, do you know that?" Nika laughed as she drove us towards Betty's all-night diner.

"I can't believe I did that," I gasped, my heart still booming away. I was still clutching the shampoo bottle and in the dull light of the car, I couldn't quite read what brand it was.

Opening the door to Betty's diner we were greeted with a warm, delicious waft of sickly-sweet cinnamon mixed with coffee. It was like a tonic, and I allowed it to wash over me and fill my lungs before I took a step further inside. Picking a table in the back corner, away from the only three other customers in the diner, we took our seats and awaited Tommo's arrival.

I knew all too well that he would be beyond furious with me, and he was right to be. What I had done was to go completely off plan and put myself and possibly the others, in danger. It was a completely stupid and reckless thing to do, but hopefully it was worth it.

Tommo soon marched in and slumping himself opposite me, shrugged his shoulders and shook his head. "Care to explain yourself then?" he asked, still clearly furious.

Just then a young dark-haired waitress, chewing gum, came to take our order while she poured us cups of coffee, which it momentarily distracted him from his fury. Sipping on the bitter coffee I felt myself relax slightly, but feeling Tommo's and Nika's eyes upon me, it didn't last long.

"Have you got anything to say for yourself?" Tommo asked bluntly, taking a sip of his own scalding coffee. "Like 'sorry, guys; I lost my mind temporarily'?"

I knew I had messed up and gone off without thinking or even telling Tommo, but it was a spur of the moment action and it had reaped a reward.

"I had to see what was going on," I protested. "We needed to know what was in those boxes." Reaching into my jacket pocket I pulled out Bronson's cell and slid it towards Tommo. The screen was pretty smashed from where it had been hurled against the wall, but it was still working.

"Where did you get that?" Tommo hissed, looking about in case anyone else had seen it. "Is this Bronson's?"

"Well, it's one of his cells that he was talking on shortly before he threw it at a wall. Whoever called him on that, is the one putting pressure on him to use his car business as a front for their dirty dealings," I replied calmly and feeling a bit smug. "He left it on a box, and it was too good an opportunity to miss."

"Let's just hope this is a burner phone and he hasn't got a tracker on it," Tommo sighed, pinching the bridge of his nose as he tried to keep his tone calm.

I hadn't even thought about the cell phone having a tracker on it and a slight sense of fear washed over me. What had I done? I could, for all I knew, be leading Bronson and half the Chinatown thugs to the diner to massacre us all.

"Wait here," Tommo instructed firmly and headed off to the kitchen of the diner.

Nika and I both sat there perplexed and as our food arrived at the table a few minutes later, so did Tommo. In his hand was an aluminium wrapped package which he placed on the table.

"What is that?" I asked through mouthfuls of hot, sugary donuts.

"The cell," Tommo grinned. "Hopefully, it will block any tracking location on it, if it's got any."

"You. Are a genius," I grinned back, blowing him a kiss, before scoffing the rest of my donuts at lightning speed.

Keeping our voices low and our eyes on the lookout for anyone that might have followed us, I relayed what I had seen and heard at 'Princeton Motors'. Tommo was very interested in the bottle of shampoo which I had taken, which was now hiding under the passenger seat of the car.

"I highly suspect that those bottles contain liquid cocaine or similar," Tommo whispered, as he chewed on some fries. "You have probably got about $10,000 sat in Mr Lin's car at this moment."

"Are you being serious?" I coughed, looking straight at Nika and then back to Tommo, who just nodded without another word.

If Tommo was right and each bottle had roughly $10,000 of cocaine inside it, then this whole set-up of Bronson's was worth hundreds of thousands of dollars, if not more.

"Surely if there is that amount of drugs contained in each bottle, they would have armed guards watching over it night and day?" Nika scoffed.

"That would draw too much attention. The fewer people, the less suspicion, I guess," Tommo replied.

I trusted what Tommo said because, although what he sold in the dodgy bars and clubs round here was illegal, it was very small fry compared to what Bronson had going on. Tommo still knew the game and, with his contacts as well, it gave us a real insight into the dark underbelly of L.A. and how it worked. Tommo carried on by telling us how operations such as this would be moved from business to business every few months, to keep it from being discovered by law enforcement.

"So, what do we do now?" Nika asked, calmly. "It's clear this guy is up to his neck with the Chinatown guys, but what does that mean for us?"

I honestly didn't know. We had discovered one huge drug dealing operation and there was potential for us to make thousands of dollars from just one bottle of 'shampoo'. We also had Bronson's cell and whatever information it contained could prove very useful to us, if only we could unlock it. A brainwave suddenly entered my sugar filled mind; we could take the cell to Petra. She, of all people would be able to hack into it and give us access to any juicy details it contained. So far, she had proven herself to be loyal and trustworthy, she was the obvious 'go to' person for something like this.

"How about we get someone to hack the phone and see what we find on it?" I suggested to Nika and Tommo.

"Petra?" Tommo nodded. "Good thinking. We need to get it to her quickly though, in case my signal-jamming trick with the foil doesn't work".

"Who is Petra?" Nika questioned, I had forgotten she had never met her.

"She's part of the team. I will explain in the car." I replied, quickly texting Petra to see if we could drop the cell straight over to her.

Petra messaged back almost instantly, and we agreed to meet outside a liquor store not far from 'Nano Bites'. As Nika and I pulled up to the kerb, Petra walked up to my window, and I passed her the foil wrapped cell through the window.

"I can have it done for you by tomorrow morning hopefully," Petra nodded, stuffing the cell into her inside jacket pocket. "It won't take long to access it, but I just need to hack into the tracker, if it has one, and disable it."
"You are literally a star." I grinned. "Oh, by the way, this is Nika, she is part of the team now."

Petra reached in through the window and shook hands with Nika. "Nice to meet you," She grinned, before saluting to me and disappearing into the dull glow of the streetlights. Turning towards me she added "Great job with Gavin, by the way! My friend couldn't praise you enough, no charge for the cell phone hack," She winked at me.

Petra's words were a boost to my confidence, but what I was really hoping for was for the cell to reveal something we could use against Bronson. Something that would get us the vengeance we needed and help his poor wife escape him for good.

Chapter Seventeen

I had kept in contact with Bronson's wife through messages on my burner phone. I hadn't told her about us staking out his business, or any other details. To be honest, I just felt like I needed to keep an eye on her. Having been assaulted at the hands of Bronson, it troubled me greatly that she was trapped in the same house with him, night after night, with him watching every move she made.

    I hadn't told Nika or Tommo yet that I had taken myself off one evening and staked out the Prince residence by myself, just to see how bad things were. I was supposed to be at home resting after the incident at the 'Blue Tiger' bar, but not knowing if Bronson's wife, Keira, was telling the truth was eating at me. I had snuck up on the house and squatted down by the kitchen window. I had gone wearing one of my long black wigs and a baseball cap just in case I was spotted, but I wasn't. It hadn't taken me long to realise that Bronson had his wife in a grip of fear. What I witnessed horrified me and left me sick to the pit of my stomach. Bronson was not only physically abusing his wife but emotionally as well. After twenty minutes of hearing him taunt his wife with sickening comments about her looks and watching him hold her hand over a lit stove ring, until she begged for mercy, I knew this animal needed all hell released upon him. It needed to happen sooner, rather than later.

***

Petra had arranged to meet me the following morning, next door at 'The Kettle Café' to discuss what she had found on the phone. Mr Lin had reserved me a table and I arrived a few minutes before our arranged time, so I could give Mr Lin the floral table arrangements I had made up for him. They had been part of our arrangement for allowing me to use the Mr Lin's car as a run-around. I had gone with a yellow and green look this time, which had almost an exotic theme to them, with a mix of lemon leaf, mokara orchids and hala leaves, in small jelly jars, wrapped with hessian and lace.

When Petra arrived, I ordered us black coffees and slices of sweet caramel cake. After Lucy had fetched us our order, I waited eagerly for Petra to tell me what she had found on the cell.

"Well let's just say that this guy needs to up his cell security, this was one of the easiest phones to hack and there was a lot of personal data on here." Petra tutted as she passed the cell across the table to me.

"What sort of personal data?" I asked, my mind eager for more information.

"This must be his main cell, it is linked to his emails and even a couple of bank accounts," Petra explained, raising her eyebrows as she slid a thick brown paper envelope towards me. "I took the liberty of downloading a few months' worth of account statements pretty smartish, before he realises his cell has gone missing and changes his passwords."

I bet he's pretty pissed off that he lost his phone and I wonder if he searched through all those boxes thinking it had fallen into one? Bronson was clearly a bit of a knucklehead and if his cell contained access to his bank accounts, what else had he left on there for us to find?

"Do you have a list of his last calls, texts, emails?" I asked Petra, screwing up my face in anticipation for her to say "No."

"Of course! It's all in the envelope." She winked as she forked a mouthful of cake into her glossy, lip lined mouth.

"You literally are the best, thank you." I gushed, passing an envelope of my own under the table and onto her lap. I always paid Petra well, her skills had helped me out more than a few times and I wanted it to stay that way.

"Like I said last night – This one's on the house, for my friend's little Gavin matter." Petra lectured, with mock-offence.

My appreciation was written all over my face, "At least let me pick up the bill for the coffees and cake?" I countered. Petra hesitated, then nodded her agreement with a smile.

With Tommo, Nika and Petra, I really had the makings of a great little team, I thought to myself.

What Petra had found out from the cell would, I was sure, prove invaluable to us in bringing Bronson down successfully. All we needed to do now was study the bank accounts and emails, then work out what to do next. I was sure that Tommo would be able to find out about the numbers listed on the call logs and find who else Bronson was mixed up with.

Heading back to 'Lily's', with the envelope tucked safely inside my jacket, I was keen to bring Nika up to speed with what we had retrieved from the cell phone. When I reached the store, I found her busily making up a personalised bouquet for an elderly woman. As I brushed past her, we made eye contact and I gave her a broad smile and a nod, indicating that we had what we wanted.

Not wanting to leave the envelope lying around, I made my way up to the apartment and slid it in between a pile of soft sweaters in my wardrobe, hiding it from sight. I would have to wait for this evening to get a proper look at what the account printouts and emails revealed.

***

It was past 9pm when Tommo, Nika and I managed to meet to look through the account printouts and emails. One of the accounts was from a bank I didn't recognise, and it soon became clear that this was an offshore account, which contained a large amount of money. The figures being transferred into the account were sizable, but it was unclear where they were actually coming from. I suspected they were payments from the Chinatown criminals, but Tommo wasn't so sure.

"I reckon these payments are from one of his other accounts and he is syphoning money off to this account as a bit of a back-up plan," Tommo suggested, gruffly. "I would have a back-up or escape plan too, if I was caught up in what he is up to?"

Nika and I nodded in agreement. It did make sense that Bronson was preparing to bolt with a lot of money, leaving everything behind including his business and any debts. I very much doubted that Kiera knew any of this, so would be left with nothing, in the wake of his departure, and potentially at the mercy of very bad people.

Tommo had done a lot of digging to find out who Bronson was actually in business with and found out it was the Hulong family that had him in their grip. They were a long-established family with links to the Triads. It turned out the Hulong family had a lengthy history of drug smuggling, extortion and even more terrifying, human trafficking.

Nika and I looked at one another and a chill passed between us. This was getting more daunting by the minute. I had effectively stolen drugs from the Hulong enterprise when I took the bottle of shampoo.

"What did you do with the bottle of shampoo?" I asked Tommo, my throat suddenly feeling dry.

"I took a sample of it to a friend of mine and he is testing it to see exactly what it contains and what sort of money it's worth, if it is liquid cocaine. I should hear back from him tonight. Don't worry, I didn't let on where I got it from," Tommo replied, a look of concern crossing his face as well now.

"What if they realise they're a bottle short?" Nika asked, suddenly. "Surely if Tommo is right about the value of those bottles, they will be counting each and every one?" Nika was right in as much as the thought of them realising some of their supply was missing, made me feel like I wanted to throw up. I had been so reckless and stupid taking it, I could have put us all in grave danger.

"Look, ladies, you just need to keep cool and calm, okay?" Tommo replied firmly. "You said there were hundreds of bottles, right, Velvet?" Watching me nod, he continued. "If he is having regular deliveries of this stuff, a few times each week, I would guarantee that it is then going on to somewhere else higher up the chain. 'Princeton Motors' is just a drop-off point and with so many boxes and changes of hands, a missing bottle would probably be accepted as an accident or such. Plus, no one knows you were there as far as we know, so the only persons to get the blame, if they do realise a bottle is missing, would be the van drivers and this Bronson bloke."

Tommo's comments did ease my worrying slightly, but there were a lot of what ifs. What if someone had seen me? What if the CCTV was recording? What if the phone was tracked? What if there was suddenly a knock at the door or a Molotov cocktail thrown through the window of the store?

Almost as if he was reading my mind, Tommo reached across the table and took my hand in his, squeezing it hard. "If they were coming for you, they would have been here by now," He smiled, gently.

I wasn't sure if I believed him. I had no choice but to hope that so far, we were in the clear with the Hulong family.

Getting up from my seat I offered to make everyone coffee, but as I stood in my little kitchen, filling the mugs, my burner phone began to vibrate on the countertop with a call waiting to be answered. I recognised the number immediately as being Keira Prince, Bronson's wife.

Nika had spotted my face change as I looked at the phone and, before she could ask me what the matter was, the call ended. Within a few seconds, a voicemail came through and I put it on speaker, placing the phone in the centre of the table for us all to hear.

The line was crackling so badly I could barely make out what Keira was saying, but she sounded desperately terrified. Through her sobs I could just about make out that she had no one else to call, that Bronson was taking her somewhere and that he was going to kill her. In the background I could hear a smashing sound and then, after a last blood-curdling scream, the line went dead.

Chapter Eighteen

Without a word to the others, I grabbed my car keys and ran downstairs, closely followed by Nika and Tommo, who were yelling at me to stop, but I blanked them. As I fumbled to get in the car, Tommo grabbed my arm and spun me around.

"What are you doing Velvet? You don't even know where they live?" he growled. "There is nothing we can do."

"I know where they live and I know what car he drives," I cried, yanking myself free and leaping into the driver's seat. Nika had leapt in the passenger seat, and we span off, leaving Tommo with his hands on his head looking like he didn't know what to do.

"How the hell do you know where they live?" Nika questioned me as we sped along the streets and highways to where Kiera and Bronson lived.

"I spied on them once, when this all started," I replied, my voice raspy and panicked. "I needed to know that Kiera was genuine about not being able to escape him, so I went and watched them at home one night after he attacked me. It was awful! He is awful and I honestly believe her when she says he is going to kill her."

"Okay, take a breath and slow down just a bit, or we aren't going to make it there without killing ourselves at this rate," Nika pleaded. "What car does she have? Do you know where they might be headed?"

I shook my head.

What I did know was that my gut feeling was screaming that, if we didn't find Keira quickly, it would be too late. Nearing their house, I could see, parked on the driveway, was Bronson's silver Mercedes; Keira's small red car was missing, and the house was in darkness. Something deep inside me made me continue down the street and onto the backroads leading away from the city, into the hills.

"We are looking for a small red coupe," I told Nika. "I'm just guessing they came this way, but I could be totally wrong." Continuing along the now less used highways, we scanned the hillsides for any sign of headlights. But there was just blackness, apart from the odd dimly lit shack by the roadside.

In my head I was desperately trying to think of anything I had seen, on their social media posts, that would give me any clue as to where Bronson could be headed. And then it came to me. On one of their posts, they had a photo of themselves at a beauty spot, high in the hills, that overlooked part of the city. The view was incredible, and Keira had commented about it being a place where she felt at total peace. I was sure that's where Bronson was headed, and we weren't far from it now.

"Up there!" Nika yelled suddenly, pointing to headlights in the far distance. Turning the car's headlights off, I used the bright moonlight to guide us up to the beauty spot known locally as 'The Overlook.' Sure enough, I caught sight of red taillights and pulled to a stop a short distance away, before sprinting from the car, with Nika following closely behind.

"That's Keira's car for sure." I whispered to Nika as we crouched behind some scrubby thorn covered bushes that lined the edge of the parking spot. The city lights glowed from the edge of the drop off that fell sharply away, in cliff like formation. We could see Bronson sat in the car and, as we inched closer, he got out, then reached inside and proceeded to drag what looked like an unconscious Keira into the driver's seat.

"What the hell is he doing? Is she alive?" Nika hissed, her eyes wide with panic.
I instantly knew what he was about to do.

"He's going to push the car over the edge with her in it," I gasped, my throat tightening as I forced the words out. "He is trying to make it look like suicide."

"We have to do something. We can't just sit here and watch while he kills her." Nika cried as she tried to keep her voice quiet.

Just then, headlights came up behind us and we dived to the floor, out of sight. The vehicle, a black SUV, circled the car park and paused by Bronson. I could hear a conversation between the driver and Bronson, and as the SUV pulled out again, Bronson was gone.

Watching the taillights disappear into the darkness, Nika and I ran for Keira's car. The doors were firmly locked and Kiera's pale face was pressed against the glass of the window. A groaning and creaking from the car made me suddenly realise that Bronson had released the handbrake. He'd positioned the car at such an angle that any movement inside the car would be enough to send it rolling down, over the edge of the cliff face.

"We need something to jam under the wheels to stop it rolling forward," I yelled at Nika, as I saw Keira begin to come round inside the car.

Nika ran off to find a log, or branch, or anything we could jam under the front tyres, in an attempt to stop it moving.

"Keira, if you can hear me, don't move." I pleaded through the glass as I felt the car move slightly again. "You mustn't move an inch. Just stay still."

Nika came back, dragging a large branch and together we positioned it under the car's front tyres. In a split second, I picked up a rounded rock from the ground and smashed at the glass with it until it shattered. Scrabbling for the door handle, which was partially blocked by Keira's slumped body, I released the door and, placing my hands under her arms, wrenched her small frame free from the vehicle.

Nika helped me to drag Kiera a short distance from the car, as she started to mumble words, we sat her up and supported her as she came to.

"Where am I?" Keira mumbled, reaching up with her hand to feel a large lump on the front of her head, where Bronson had knocked her unconscious.

"It's okay. You're safe now," I whispered into her soft hair as I hugged her tightly.

"What do we do now?" Nika asked, crouching down to examine Kiera's head wound. "Call the cops?"

I shook my head and stood up, leaving Nika to support Kiera as she got to her feet. Looking back inside the car, I recovered Keira's brown leather handbag and chucked it to her feet. Shutting the door, I walked round to the front of the vehicle and dragged the branch out of the way. Without a word to Nika or Keira, I went behind the car and, pulling my sleeves over my hands, I pushed the rear bumper, just enough, to send the car forwards and down over the cliff face. It crashed and scraped its way down over the rocks while I walked back to Nika, who stood open mouthed at what I had just done. Behind me, the car had reached its final destination and burst into flames on impact in the valley far below.

"What the hell Velvet? Why did you do that?" Nika yelled, completely confused by my actions.

"Well, Bronson wanted Keira dead and now he thinks she *is*. We can use it to our advantage," I explained, as I approached Keira who, although was now on her feet, looked completely spaced out.

"We need to get her out of here now," I told Nika sharply, the explosion would probably have been seen by God knows who, and the place would soon be swarming with cars and cops. Nika just nodded and ran back to where my car was hidden out of sight.

With Keira safely on the back seat, we headed down the long winding track towards the highway. I had kept my lights off, just in case Bronson, and whoever it was that picked him up, were still about. My thinking was they would have seen or heard the car explode and would assume the job was done and Keira was dead.

Pulling out into the stream of traffic on the highway, we all took a collective deep breath of relief. Ahead of us I could make out the flashing lights of a cop car, but they pulled off the highway further up and headed in the opposite direction to 'The Overview'. I could hear Kiera sniffing on the back seat and checking in the rear-view mirror to see if she was okay, our eyes met.

"Who are you?" Kiera asked meekly, in between sniffing and crying. It was then that I remembered that she didn't have a clue who we were. We had never met, only messaged via the 'Black Bloom' website or my burner phone.

Nika and I exchanged glances and finding a suitable place to park up, I pulled the car to a stop, just off the highway. I figured that now Kiera had seen our faces, we might as well tell her our real names and who we really were.

"I'm the one you rang when you realised your husband was going to hurt you. My name is Velvet, and this is Nika," I smiled, twisting in my seat to hold out my hand, which she took gently and shook, still uneasy about me.

"So, you're the one who I hired to try and honey-trap him? The one he attacked?" she gasped, suddenly wincing at the pain in her head.

"Yep, that's me, but before we get down to the who, why's and where's, I think we best get that head of yours looked at." I suggested, feeling the pain she was in.

"No, honestly, I'm fine," Kiera insisted. "It's not the first time he has knocked me out and luckily I'm a fast healer."

"Well, let us at least get you cleaned up and get an ice pack on that lump. We obviously can't take you back to your house because Bronson will know you're alive," I replied.

"She could stay with me?" Nika proposed. "I have a comfy couch, and no one would know to look for her there."

Nika's apartment was on the second floor and when she opened the door, a warm glow of light filtered out. Bright coverings hung on the walls and ornate glass lamps set the scene for a comfy stay. Helping Kiera to Nika's cushion covered sofa, I let her settle and gather her thoughts, while Nika and I chatted in the kitchen in hushed voices.

"So, what now?" Nika asked bluntly. "I'm happy for her to stay here for a while, but she is effectively a dead person until the cops check the car wreckage and don't find a body."

"Judging by that explosion, I would imagine there's not much of anything left down there by now," I shrugged. "It will take the cops a while to identify the owner of the car, if they ever can. I suspect, if they don't find any human remains, they will probably just put it down to being a stolen then dumped, vehicle."

"I never thought of that," Nika mused. "You literally think of everything."

Keira sat slumped on Nika's sofa with a sweet cup of coffee in one hand a bag of ice to her head with the other. We started to unravel what had happened in the lead up to her desperate phone call to me. It transpired that Keira knew very little about who Bronson was involved with, but she knew about the drugs and money laundering to an extent. By the sounds of it, she had ploughed a lot of her own money into the business and the house, money she had inherited, after the death of her parents.

"I think the only reason Bronson married me, was because he knew I had a large inheritance and no one else. He was charming and loving, at first and it was very easy to fall under his spell. As soon as we were married, his behaviour started to change and, before I knew it, my money was all but gone. I only have minimal shares in the businesses and half the house left," She explained sadly.

Keira was indeed a victim in this whole matter and my heart nearly broke for her, seeing her sat there, bruised and broken. I knew what it was like to lose your family, but I was lucky in the fact that I hadn't come across, or been trapped by, a person like Bronson. I quite easily could have been. Men like him preyed on vulnerable girls like Keira, not caring what hurt or destruction they left in their wake.

"I had no choice but to try and trap him cheating on me," Keira suddenly said, her eyes rimmed with tears and remorse. "I was so desperate to be able to get some money and get away, but it all just kept going wrong and people got hurt because of me."

I looked straight at Nika and shook my head. I didn't want her to tell Keira about her friend being attacked so badly, not now anyway.

"So, what happened tonight? Did he just snap?" I asked, carefully. "How did you know he was planning on killing you?"

Kiera blew her nose in a tissue and then placed the ice bag back on her head. "He came home suddenly, in furious mood for some reason, and found me going through some of his files. He went ballistic and dragged me by the hair to the bedroom and locked me in. I hammered on the door for him to let me out. I was screaming for help from anyone, but no one came. Then I got worried he would come in after me again, so I slid down to the floor with my back against the door and tried to hear what he was up to. I really wish I hadn't."

"Why was that? Was there someone else there?" I asked gently, handing her a glass of brandy Nika fetched for her.

After taking a large sip Keira continued, "I was sat there, literally holding my breath, trying to listen and that's when I heard him talking to someone on the phone. His voice was really agitated and loud so I could hear him quite clearly. "Kiera took another large sip of her brandy and then, with a deep breath, she steeled herself to tell us what happened next. "I have no idea who he was talking to, but he was telling them to pick him up from 'The Overlook' in an hour's time. He was shouting down the phone saying, "Just do as I say and don't ask any questions. It will look like an accident".

I slid down beside Keira amongst the soft cushions and put my arm around her. "You are doing really well," I whispered into her hair pulling her close, feeling her gaunt frame shiver with shock.

"After hearing what he said, I just knew he was going to try and kill me. He has threatened it so many times before and I knew he was desperate to get me out of the way, after what I had just seen in the files." Kiera sniffed, as she emptied the rest of her glass.

"What did you see in the files that made him so mad?" Nika asked, topping up Kiera's glass with another generous shot of brandy.

"They were statements from a bank I didn't recognise and there were thousands and thousands of dollars in them. I had found them in an old briefcase he'd hidden in the wine cellar. I watched him go down there a few times, he always kept the stair door locked and kept the key with him. I managed to use a screwdriver to remove the door handle as I was convinced he had cash stashed down there. I was going to take it and run if he did. Unfortunately, he came home and found me with the files."

"They were statements for an offshore account. We managed to hack his cell, so we already know he is up to his neck in trouble," I told her bluntly, not knowing how much she knew about her husband's involvement with the Hulong family.

"How the hell did you get hold of his phone?" Kiera asked, pulling herself away from me slightly. "Who are you really? Are you undercover detectives or something?"

"No, we are definitely nothing to do with any police force and it's probably best that you don't know how we got his phone." I laughed, imagining Nika and me in cop's uniforms.

"He has more than one phone, I take it?" Nika asked.

Kiera nodded. "He had at least two that I know of, a personal one and a work one."

"So, what happened after you heard him talking on the cell?" I asked gently, wondering if I dared listen to what she was about to tell us.

"Well, after hearing what he was saying on the cell, I tried to barricade the door with furniture to stop him getting in. He must have guessed or heard what I was doing and after he had unlocked the door, he started ramming it with his shoulder. I managed to speed dial your number and tried to run to the window, but he had already burst through the door and grabbed me by the hair again as I tried to get the latch open. He then started to punch me repeatedly in the head and I started to lose consciousness. I next remember being dragged backwards by my arms into the kitchen and what I thought was water being poured on my face. I then realised it was vodka as it began to burn my eyes. He sat on my chest and continued to pour more vodka in my mouth, I gasped for air and then, I don't remember much else. I guess he knocked me clean out and when I woke, you guys were there, getting me out of the car."

"Oh, my God." I sighed, realising that Keira had escaped death by literally seconds. "No wonder you have been so desperate to escape him."

Kneeling in front of her, I took both of her hands in mine. They felt ice cold. "You are safe now, okay? And I can promise you, that piece of scum is going to get what's coming to him."

Keira nodded, a slight sparkle returning to her dark rimmed eyes. "I want to help you. I don't want to be the victim anymore. He plied me with alcohol, tried to push me off the cliff in my car to make it look like I was drunk and killed myself. Bronson thinks I am dead, at the bottom of the ravine, but I'm not and I have never felt more alive."

Chapter Nineteen

Leaving Keira to rest under the watchful eye of Nika, I drove home, thoughts of what just happened, or nearly happened, to Keira swimming fresh in my head, replaying every detail, as it was on a playback loop. Who the hell was the guy in the SUV? He must be an associate or friend of Bronson, someone who was equally as caught up in this as he was.

I had spoken to Tommo on the phone before I left and filled him in on what had happened. He had been out of his mind with worry, understandably, and for everything I relayed to him I got an ear-bashing's worth back. It was perfectly justified, of course, because yet again, I had been reckless and this time I had put Nika in danger too. Although she hadn't of needed to jump in the car with me, I was damn pleased she did. My actions had been reckless at best, but we had saved a woman's life tonight and that outweighed everything, in my opinion.

We had arranged to meet the next evening to go over what we now knew. Tommo had hinted that he had some leads on the cell numbers that were in Bronson's contact list but wasn't keen to chat about it over a call. What happened to Keira now was playing on my mind big time, but she was right in saying that she could be useful to us now that Bronson thought she was dead. What part she played next would have to be thought about and considered carefully.

Lying wrapped up in the comfort of my duvet, I tossed and turned endlessly. Sleep was going to evade me tonight and I needed a distraction. Pulling on some loose-fitting slacks and a fleece-lined hoodie, I plodded barefoot downstairs to the store. Flicking on the main lights, I began rearranging the displays and wiping down the already clean shelves, until they glistened and gleamed that little bit brighter. I then turned my attention to the heavy, clothbound, order book that sat on the store's glass-topped counter. We had a couple of orders that week for more funeral flowers, so to be ultra-efficient, I started making lists for the flower market and ordering anything unusual the clients had requested.

Funeral orders, along with wedding flowers, were the bread and butter for the business because there was always one or the other happening. The funeral trade was one that never had a season and it plodded on from winter to summer, on and on relentlessly. I had provided flowers for the very old and flowers for the very young and it was a job I took a lot of pride in. Flowers have a magical way of evoking emotion no matter the circumstances and they can offer light, in even the darkest of situations. It was 4am before I headed back upstairs and climbed fully dressed into my crumpled bed, sleep now flooding over me like an anaesthetic, I fell instantly asleep.

***

I woke the next morning as if I had a hangover or the flu, my body felt stiff, and my head felt filled with feathers. Two strong cups of coffee and a croissant later and eventually I felt human enough to head downstairs to open the store, ready for Nika to arrive. I had given her the option of staying home today to keep an eye on Keira, but she insisted she was fine, and Keira was just going to remain on the sofa, watching TV quietly, while Nika was gone. I got the feeling that Nika didn't want to have to babysit Keira, so I didn't argue and replied, saying I would look forward to seeing her soon.

"My, my, someone has been busy," Nika chuckled as she removed her white-rimmed sunglasses and observed the now gleaming shop. "I take it you didn't get much sleep last night?"

"I needed a distraction," I shrugged. "So, how is Keira this morning?"

"Her face is many shades of purple and blue, but she seems okay in herself. I left her drinking a glass of juice and eating a bowl of cereal as she insisted that I came into work," Nika replied, pulling on her thick cotton apron.

"I expect she just wants some time to get things straight in her head after last night," I sighed. "It's not every day your crazy husband tries to throw you off a cliff."

"Yeah, I totally get her wanting some quiet time and I have left her our numbers in case she wants to call us." Nika agreed. "Do we know what happened to her cell phone? The one she called you on?"

I hadn't even given a thought to the fact Keira called me from her own cell last night and that it would still have my burner phone number on it.

"From what I heard when she called me, it sounded like the phone had hit something hard and then cut off, so I imagined Bronson had smashed it to smithereens," I suggested to Nika, but I couldn't be sure. If he still had Kiera's phone, he could redial the number she last dialled and that would lead him straight to my burner phone.

I had switched my burner phone off last night, so I didn't have to deal with any messages coming from the 'Black Blooms' website until I was ready. Fishing it out from my jacket pocket, I switched it on. After a couple of minutes, a message pinged its way through, and I looked at Nika. "What if it's him?" I whispered, as if Bronson might already be listening in.

"Only one way to find out," Nika replied, walking to my side so she could see the message.

To our relief, the message was what seemed to be a legitimate job from the 'Black Blooms' website, asking about ordering some 'pink peonies' for their boss. I replied back, asking them what they actually wanted doing and suggested a humiliating phone call. I included a one-off fee quote and awaited their response.

Half an hour later a reply came back, giving me brief details of who they wanted to prank and why. It was pretty much the same story with many of the 'pink peonies' orders that came through; a disgruntled employee wanting a little bit of their own back on a sour boss. For $50 I agreed to call his office, talk to the boss's secretary, and inform them the boss, Mr Thacker, had a positive result from his STD tests, carried out the previous week. The twist was that Mr Thacker was rumoured to be having an affair with said secretary, and by the sounds of it, the employee had felt some justice was needed.

"So, how about you take this one?" I grinned at Nika, my eyebrows twitching up and down playfully.

"I would just love to." Nika grinned back, her eyes widening and her face lighting up.

Within another half an hour, the $50 had been paid into my 'special account' and Nika was dialling the offices of Thacker and Spout realtors. We had informed the client that the call would be made at 11am so that they and anyone else could be in position to listen in.

Nika, adjusting her slender frame on one of the leather-topped stools in the back storeroom, cleared her throat and prepared for her first job as prank caller.

"Good morning, this is Vivian calling from the Madley Clinic with the results of Mr Thacker's tests he had done last week." Nika purred, putting on a polished tone that had me covering my mouth to stifle a laugh.

"Oh dear, he is in a meeting? Okay. Well, it is quite important we speak to him as his condition is very contagious," She continued. "What sort of clinic are we? Well, I am not sure if I should say?"

Nika was now trying to desperately keep her composure, I marvelled at the way she kept her tone of voice levelled and matter of fact.

"Okay! Well, I can see from our notes that he is happy for results to be given to a third party if he is indisposed, so that's not a problem. Here at the Madley Clinic, we specialise in the early detection of sexually transmitted diseases and their treatment." Nika's eyes started widening and she shifted on the stool as she steeled herself to continue. "Well yes, I am afraid that Mr Thacker's results have come back positive, and we are putting up a prescription for a strong cream that will need to be applied three times a day to the areas affected." Nika explained, while I held on to the counter to stop myself from falling down with laughter.

"Oh dear, is everything okay? Hello?" Nika held the phone up to her face and laughed. "She appears to have hung up!"

When I had stopped howling with laughter, I held up my hand to Nika for a high five and we both dissolved into fits of laughter again.

"You are a complete natural at this," I howled, wondering what the hell was now happening in the offices of 'Thacker and Spout'. "That was brilliant."

Nika got down from the stool where she was perched and did a little curtsey. "I can see why you do this," She giggled. "That was the best fun ever, and $50 for three minutes work is not a bad return."

We spent the rest of the afternoon spontaneously bursting into laughter over the phone call and Nika was up for doing as many as I wanted her to do. With everything done in the store and only an hour until closing, Nika headed home to check on Kiera. Tommo and I would meet her at her place later to discuss Bronson.

I still had thoughts of what we could do to him swimming in my mind, but most of the ideas were overcomplicated and dangerous. We needed something simple but effective and that wasn't going to be easy to figure out.

Hearing my store doorbell ring, I left the storeroom, where I was stacking empty boxes, to find Mr Lin standing at the counter with a white cardboard box held in his gentle hands.

"Hello Velvet, we had these few cakes left over today and we didn't want to waste them, so thought you might like them?" he beamed, bobbing his head in his usual overly-polite fashion.

"Mr Lin, you are quite wonderful," I smiled, taking the box from him and peering inside at the sweet treasure that lay within.

Bidding him 'good night', I locked the door behind him and went up to the apartment to take a shower. I had a couple of hours before I met with everyone at Nika's and there was a little errand I wanted to run first.

Pulling on some jeans and a pale blue pullover I drove down to the local drug store and filled a basket with face creams, make up and self-care items. I also picked up some multipacks of underwear, as I figured Kiera would want her own things so to speak, and I hoped that make-up would make her feel better.

Nika had sent me a message as soon as she got home to say that Keira was fine, just quiet, which was to be expected. She luckily seemed none the worse from her ordeal physically, but I had no doubt that her mind was full of what ifs and why's. Rummaging through my wardrobe, I put together a bundle of my lesser-used soft sweaters, simple t-shirts and some sweatpants. Kiera was similar to my build, maybe a little more petite, but I was sure these few clothes would be enough to tide her over for now.

Pulling up outside Nika's apartment block, I opened the trunk of the car and heaved out the bags of goodies for Kiera.

"Need a hand with those?" A familiar voice asked from behind me.

"Well now, that would be wonderful. I always said you were a gentleman, Tommo, no matter what other people say." I grinned, turning round to greet him with a kiss on his stubbly cheek and passing him the bags.

Nika and Keira had been busy in the kitchen when we arrived, the intoxicating smell of something delicious filled the room from what appeared to be something bubbling away in a large pot, on the stove top.

"I have made us a pot of beef chilli for tonight," Nika smiled as she handed out large white plates to us all.

Squeezing ourselves around her small dining table, we took turns to spoon out helpings of chilli and white rice. After a few spoonsful, I turned my attention to Kiera, who was tending to push her food around her plate without putting much into her mouth.

"So how are you feeling today, Kiera?" I asked gently. I knew it was probably a stupid question, but I had to try and get her talking.

"I'm okay, thanks." She smiled back, but I could see her eyes were a bit lifeless and her posture hunched.

"I bought you some things to keep you going," I replied, gesturing to the bags piled by the door. "There is everything from underwear to makeup in there and if you need anything else, please don't hesitate to ask."
"You are so kind," Keira sighed, and I could see tears beginning to fill in her eyes. The sparkle that she had yesterday and the determination to help deal with Bronson. had all but gone.

"Keira, I know this is all a bit much at the moment, but you need to remember that you are safe now and I promise with all my heart that you will get your life back," I told her firmly and I meant it.

"But I have no one, no family, no real friends, just wives of Bronson's acquaintances who are more interested in Botox and tennis clubs. I lost my father when I was eleven and my mother when I was seventeen; then I worked in restaurants and bars," She explained sadly, her voice wavering. "I managed to access my inheritance when I was eighteen but still continued working in one of the bars. That's when I met Bronson. I guess I'm just one of those people who is alone and unlucky all their life."

"You are not alone now, you have us," I pointed out, reaching across the table for her hand and squeezing it. "All we have to do now is put our heads together to plan what we do next and that is what tonight is all about."

With the food all finished and cleared away to the kitchen, we gathered back around the table, and I asked Tommo to explain what he had found on Bronson's contact list. Tommo confirmed a few of the numbers matched those used by members of the Hulong family, whereas others were untraceable and were more than likely burner phones.

"There were some interesting text messages though." Tommo explained bringing out the cell from his back pocket and tapping the screen. "There are messages from a contact named Rayne, who seems to talk in complete gibberish, but I am assuming it is code."

Keira took the phone and peered at the messages Tommo had put up on the screen.
"I don't recognise the name but then again Bronson never really told me anything anyway. I used to overhear him talking on the phone a lot and some of these words do sound familiar. Sorry, I don't know in what context," Keira shrugged.

"What words do you recognise or think you have heard before?" I asked.

"Well, the one word that sticks out most is Enihs, I think he pronounced it like the girls name, Ines? Bronson used to talk on the phone about what time Ines or Enihs would be arriving for her meeting and how many boxes were required this time." Keira continued.

I took the phone from her and read the messages myself over and over. The sentences were short and a mix of spelt out numbers and misspelt words. It really did read like someone had a hard job spelling, but it was definitely code.

"How do you spell Enihs?" Nika asked, grabbing a pen and a scrap of paper to write on.

"ENIHS" I told her as I watched her write it down.

"Do you guys remember the name of the brand on the shampoo bottle you had from the car place?" Nika asked, her eyes narrowing as if her mind was working overtime.

"Hang on, I took a photo of it on my burner," I replied, taking it out and scrolling through it until I found what I was searching for. "Okay, here we are, it was just simply called Shine."

Nika laughed a little and caught my eyes with a glittery stare. "And what does SHINE spell backwards?" She asked, raising her eyebrows as she started to write ENIHS.

"Surely it can't be that simple?" Tommo scoffed, taking the phone back before shaking his head. "Well, I'll be damned that does make sense."

"Nice one, Nika. I can't believe I didn't think of that," I tutted, rolling my eyes. "It seems so obvious now. Whoever this Rayne is must be the one organising the drop-offs of the 'shampoo'."

Tommo was yet to tell us the result of what was actually in the bottles of 'shampoo', but I was already pretty sure I knew what they contained. "So do we have it confirmed now, Tommo, that it was liquid cocaine in the bottles?" I asked him.

"My source can confirm, that particular bottle of shampoo, indeed contained almost pure liquid cocaine, with a value in excess of $20,000, and he said that was a modest estimate," Tommo replied, folding his arms across his chest.

"Holy crap!" I breathed, not knowing what else to say.

Keira sat dumbfounded. She had told us she knew about his involvement with drugs and money laundering, but clearly had no idea of the scale in which her husband was involved in the drug business. I wondered if this revelation would send her over the edge.

"So do we think this Rayne person could be the one Keira overheard Bronson talking to on his cell last night, and the one that came to get him from 'The Overlook?" I asked the others.

"It could be, yes," Tommo replied. "A call was made from this cell to that number around the time Keira told us, there was another number called as well, but that was untraceable. "My bet is this Rayne person is Bronson's right-hand man."

"Do you recognise the name at all, or do you remember anyone coming to the house who could be this Rayne guy?" I asked Keira.

"Bronson never really had any friends or business partners over to the house. Everything was done at the car business. He was so careful not to let me in on any of his dealings, whether they were legitimate, or not. I think he knew I was on to something, and he was extra cautious," Keira replied, shaking her head slowly. "I am so sorry I can't be any more help."

"Don't be silly," I smiled, squeezing her hand again. "You are better off not knowing much, trust me. Bronson might have tried to kill you sooner if you found out more."

"Yeah, that is true," Kiera sniffed, blowing her nose into a screwed-up tissue.

"So, what is our next step forward?" I asked the group. "We need to act fast before the cops recover Keira's car and Bronson realises that his wife isn't dead like he planned."

"Clearly Bronson is planning on doing a runner, away from these Hulong people and that is why he has set up these offshore accounts to funnel money from his dodgy dealings. The accounts that we accessed are proof of his intent and he clearly panicked when he came home to find Keira had discovered them. His attempt to kill her and make it look like a drunken accident were a clumsy way of trying to buy himself more time to get out," Nika mused, shaking her head, struggling to get her head around how someone could snuff out another's life, just so they could get themselves out of trouble.

"You are exactly right." I nodded. "He is hoping that the cops will run a toxicology test on Keira's body, and it will come back with high levels of alcohol in her blood stream. The cops would think she was driving under the influence and mistakenly went over the edge, or that with her mental health issues, she killed herself. I bet he is practicing how to play the shocked, grieving husband when the cops arrive to tell him of his poor wife's untimely demise."

"I also have a history of anxiety and depression which Bronson used against me whenever I called the cops about his abuse. He made me out to be a complete loony and he flipped it around, so he became the victim," Keira spat, a bit more life now starting to spark in her deep blue eyes. "The cops finding me intoxicated at the bottom of the ravine would fit nicely into his little story about me being unhinged."

Keira was starting to come back to become more involved now and this evening had been like some kind of therapy for her. I still didn't think she would be much use to us going forward, as she clearly had a vulnerable side, which could prove risky for us if things got really heated. Also, we didn't know her that well and I needed people around me I could rely on fully. The abuse she had suffered at the hands of Bronson was sure to have long term effects on her, let alone the fact that she nearly lost her life.

In the back of my mind, I did have a plan of how we could use Kiera to bring down Bronson, but it was far from polished. I wasn't keen to tell the others my idea yet because I wanted to check a few things out first, to make sure that what I had in mind had a chance of working. I needed to know what affect thinking he killed Keira was having on him and I wanted to find out more about this sidekick of his, who came to pick him up from 'The Overlook'. I needed to do a bit more of my own private investigating and get it clear in my mind how exactly we were going to proceed.

Chapter Twenty

On the way home from our meeting at Nika's apartment, I ran over in my head what I needed to do a few more times. Ideally, what I wanted to know was how, and when, Bronson was planning on bolting with an account full of dodgy money, belonging to a well-known crime family. There must be some sort of clues hidden at their house, and it must have been what Keira discovered, when Bronson walked in on her a couple of nights ago. The only way to find out what he had planned next, was to search his house, which would not be easy.

Stashed away in a small bag, on the back seat of the car, was a change of clothes. Pulling into a quiet layby, I quickly changed from my jeans and t-shirt into a pair of black sports leggings and a long-sleeved black top. I tucked my hair up into a black knitted hat, much like I had done when I went to 'Princeton Motors' a few nights ago. Bronson and Kiera's property was a ten-minute drive away, and as I drove closer, I kept my eyes peeled for a suitable place where I could leave the car. Parking up, I pulled on a light coloured, knee-length jacket and hung an empty handbag over my shoulder, to make it look like I was just coming home from an evening out.

After initially walking past their property, I confirmed to my satisfaction, that no-one was home by the lack of a vehicle in the drive and only a small light left on in the kitchen. Double checking that no one was around, I slipped down the drive and after removing my jacket and handbag, stashed them in a bush at the side of the house. Carefully and quietly, I tip-toed my way around the building, peeking into every window for any sign of life. There was nothing.

I heard voices coming from the house next door, so I pressed myself against the wall and waited. The neighbours, a middle-aged couple, paused and chatted for a few seconds on their driveway, before getting into their car and speeding off down the street. This area was pretty upmarket, and I suspected, before I came, that Bronson had a security system fitted.

Luckily, after a quick conversation with Petra, she had also managed to access the security firm's details from Bronson's phone and had given me the code for the keypad. I was all set, well, that was unless Bronson had changed the code. There was only one way to find out.

Slipping a knife blade into the back door frame, I managed to spring open the lock and quietly pushed the door open. An immediate high-pitched beeping started so I proceeded straight to the hallway where the keypad sat illuminated in green light on the wall. With everything crossed and my heart racing, I punched in the numbers and after another long beep, the alarm silenced. Letting out a long breath, I darted my eyes around the house for security cameras. I couldn't see any but that didn't mean there weren't any. I needed to be fast, find what I wanted and get out.

The house was very minimalistic, so searching all the obvious desk drawers and cupboards was easy enough, but I had found nothing of use yet. The small pen torch I brought along gave me enough light to look through any files that I found, without being obvious to anyone passing by outside. There had to be somewhere that was used to store things such as passports and jewellery. I just hadn't found it yet.

Peeking under paintings and photos on the wall, I searched for a hidden safe, but there was nothing. Bronson's home office was just full of car paperwork and apart from a small metal locked box in his desk drawer, there was nothing of any significance. After giving the small, locked box a gentle shake, I realised that it only contained what sounded like car keys so I didn't bother trying to prise it open. Shining the torch round the outskirts of the office, its beam touched upon a tiny corner of paper, sticking up from a floorboard, by the side of a wooden and glass drinks cabinet. Kneeling down, I carefully picked at it with my nails and eased it from where it was trapped. It was a passport photo of Bronson. Shining the torch under the drink's cabinet, I could see that one of the floorboards sat up slightly higher than the others and dragging the cabinet just enough to access the boards, I took out my knife and with a little effort, eased one up. At first there seemed to be nothing underneath it except darkness and dust, but lying flat on my stomach, I reached my arm in and felt around. Trying not to freak out too much about the cobwebs, that were now entwining my fingers like candyfloss, I felt the back of my hand brush against something. Easing it out with my fingers I revealed a heavy, dark green cloth bag and, after replacing the floorboard, I stood up, making my way to the marble topped desk that stood in the centre of the room.

Holding the torch in my teeth, I began fiddling with the knotted cord at the top of the bag and began to ease it open to peek at what was inside. Whatever was inside had obviously been hidden for a reason and I was praying it was what I was looking for. Suddenly, a flash of light caught my eye and to my horror, I looked up and saw a car pulling into the driveway.

Bronson was home. Shit! With my heart pounding, I dragged the drinks cabinet back into place and darted for the back door, stopping briefly at the alarm panel, to hastily punch in the code to reset it. The alarm made three short beeps before it started to reset and I dived for the back door, slinked through it, and closed it gently. Hearing the alarm's long beep, I held my breath and prayed that he hadn't heard the alarm reset tones.

Creeping my way back down the side of the house, I made my way silently along the wall until I reached a vantage point where I could see the driveway. Bronson was sat in the driver's seat talking into his cell, his head resting on his left hand. With the cloth bag tucked safely inside my jacket I waited, my breath shuddering as I tried to keep it controlled and steady.

After a few minutes, Bronson exited his car and made for the front door, giving me the opportunity to escape back onto the street and return to where I had parked the car.

Slumping into the familiar comfort of the little black car, I gathered myself and checked around to make sure that I hadn't been seen or followed. Everything was still and quiet. Pulling off my gloves with my teeth, I started to open the cloth bag again and, with the string now free, I tipped the contents onto the passenger seat. Not one, but three passports, a bundle of cash, a set of keys and finally a small black gun slid out onto the seat. A quick look at the passports revealed just what we had thought all along. The passports all had photos of Bronson, but the names and addresses were false. This was the jackpot, this was his 'get out of town' bag and now I had it.

I shoved everything back into the bag, re-tied the top and pushed it under the passenger seat. Seeing the gun had given me the chills, only because I wondered what other dark dealings it had been used for. Making my way back down the highway, my head was now filling with ideas on how I would break this to my loyal teammates; how I had crept out once again, without telling any of them my plans and yet again put myself in reckless danger. It may have been reckless and stupid, but my actions had paid off, luckily, I had now stopped Bronson escaping his dark dealings and the karma he was owed. He was going nowhere too far now I had his fake identities, and despite knowing I would get a backlash from Nika and Tommo, a little smile spread across my lips.

***

Back in the low-lit sanctuary of my apartment, I placed the cloth bag and its contents into a half-empty box of soap powder under the kitchen sink, slid it to the back of the cupboard and showered. The hot water flooded over me like a warm embrace, any remaining tension I had left after breaking into Bronson's house soon made its way down the plug hole with the soap suds.

What I had riskily done still played on my mind and, although I had been terrified of being caught, or worse, the pure thrill of what I just pulled off left me buzzing. I would be straight with Nika and Tommo tomorrow, any telling off I received would be well worth it and soon forgotten, especially when they saw what I had found.

Diving into bed with a towel wrapped around my head, I sat against the pillows and texted Tommo, telling him to meet me at my place again the following evening. I would tell Nika when she turned up for work the next morning, as that would give me a chance throughout the day to get her on my side before I announced to Tommo what I had retrieved. I wasn't a child, and I was perfectly entitled to put myself in danger if I wished, but I knew Tommo cared for me like a little sister and he would feel a little betrayed and hurt that, I had once again, not consulted him. The reason I hadn't consulted him was because he would have stopped me going and then we would not have the fake passports and gun. Yes, I could have been caught, but I wasn't, and he had to trust me to make my own decisions and take my own risks.

The run-in and beating I had taken from Bronson that night at the bar rocked me to my core, but I had come through the ordeal a stronger woman. I knew what I wanted to do with my life now and the 'Black Blooms' website was just the start of it. The thrill I got from having one over on the low-life scum that inhabited this beautiful city was like oxygen; I needed it to live now. Yes, I had to be careful, especially with guys like Bronson and the people he was mixed up with, but I wanted to get better at it and learn new skills. The vengeance game had certainly proved to be profitable and even the small jobs, like prank calls to creepy bosses, gave me a hit of satisfaction. It was a win-win game as long as I was careful and didn't get cocky.

This whole thing with Bronson and getting vengeance for what he had done to both me, Kiera and Nika's friend Monica, had gone on long enough. It wouldn't be too long before Bronson realised that someone had been in his house and relieved him of his getaway plan. I couldn't predict what his next move would be and none of us knew what was happening with the discovery and recovery of Keira's car. The cops would soon be banging on Bronson's door with news of her car, if they hadn't already, and without Keira's body being found in the vehicle, Bronson would soon know she was alive.

I wondered to myself whether he reported her missing, to try to cover his tracks as the concerned husband, or if he waited until they knocked on his door to tell them that one night she had flown into a crazy rage and fled the house, never to be seen again. Whichever way he had thought it through in his head, it was all about to come back to haunt him, but not in the way he had planned, thanks to Nika, Tommo and I. We now had his wife and his fake passports and had hopefully scuppered any future plans, for now. Bronson was no longer in the driving seat of his little plan, we were.

Chapter Twenty-One

Nika took the news of my late night, solo break pretty well. She had folded her arms across her chest, rolled those amber coloured eyes of hers and shaken her head, as I relayed my story, but she hadn't shouted at me. I presumed she was leaving that pleasure for Tommo later. In the short time we had known each other, I think she had pretty much figured me out and nothing I did really surprised her anymore. I didn't know if that was a good or bad thing.

Another wedding order had come in from a former customer, who now had his youngest daughter's wedding to pay for. She had been very specific that everything from the bridal flowers to the men's buttonholes, had to be made from roses. When Mr Lucano had first walked through my shop door two years ago, he had made it quite clear that money was no object for his daughter Isobella's wedding. So, with help from one of my stockists at the market, we put together one of the biggest orders I had ever taken on as a florist, and definitely the most profitable. Mr Lucano had given me a very generous tip too, for helping to make his daughter's day extra special, and I was hoping he might do the same again this time. I was thrilled to have him place another order and he was again a pleasure to deal with, paying up front, and giving detailed plans of what the flower arrangements should look like. I was sure that Mr Lucano was part of some sort of mafia from the way he spoke and dressed, and he fascinated me with his no nonsense approach.

A sharp wrap on the glass windowpane, of the store's door, alerted Nika and me to the presence of another large delivery of specially ordered roses from my main supplier, Karl, who I had got to know through the flower market. This size job was equally as important to him as it was to me, and he had gone out of his way to keep me overflowing with every shade of rose there was available. My little shop now looked, and smelt, like some sort of perfume advert, and I had flipped the 'Closed' notice round to stop anyone else coming in. There was simply no more room for anyone else in the shop.

Nika and I worked like a true team that day, sorting, pruning, de-leafing and packing hundreds of roses into huge glass vases, ready to be delivered to the wedding venue the next morning.

By the evening we were exhausted but, tired or not, I had to meet with Tommo to confess to what I had done at Bronson's house. The thought of him yelling at my already worn-out head was even less desirable now, but it couldn't wait any longer. With the wedding order now out of the way, we were clear to deal with Bronson.

Arriving at Nika's at 8pm that evening, I took in a long, deep breath before I tapped on the blue-painted door to announce my arrival. Nika opened the door with a broad smile and a wink, and I could see behind her, Tommo was sat talking to Keira on the couch. Keira looked different today, almost like she had gained a little meat to the delicate, bird like bones, that usually made up her frame. It was amazing how someone can transform with a bit of love and nurture. I just hoped her mental health was on its way to being repaired, too.

Nika had offered to provide the food for us this evening, but after a busy day prepping wedding flowers and clearing up, I insisted on ordering pizza. Within half an hour, we were all sat feasting on an overload of carbs, while we laughed and joked at some of Tommo's stories from years gone past. I relished the happy atmosphere while it lasted because the time was now upon me to confess to my solo mission at Keira and Bronson's house.

I had decided to just come on out with what I had done, and found, that evening in a blunt fashion, much like ripping off a band aid. However, I was sure that the earbashing I was about to be given was going to last a little bit longer. Pulling out the cloth bag from inside my jacket pocket, I set it down in the centre of the table and waited for Tommo to ask me what it was. I didn't have to wait long.

"What's that?" Tommo asked predictably, as he finished the last bite of his three-cheese pizza slice and proceeded to wipe his hands on his ripped jeans.

"I may have called into Keira's old residence," I half smiled, half grimaced.

"You may have what?" Tommo scoffed, but I knew he had heard me correctly the first time, so I waited with my teeth clenched, in a mock smile. This was it, time to be yelled at.

"Don't freak out, Tommo, I got what we needed," I sighed. "I know you hate me going rogue but some things, I just need to do on my own."

"Like get bloody injured or killed?" Tommo spat, folding his arms across his chest and shaking his head, clearly furious, like I knew he would be.

"I'm here talking to you, aren't I?" I replied in a sing-song fashion and reached out to tip the contents of the bag onto the table.

As the gun and passports spilt onto the table, I watched the colour drain once again from Keira's face. She clearly had no idea that Bronson had kept a gun in the house.

Feeling Tommo's eyes boring into me as I explained how I had got into the house, I hoped he would soon turn from being furious to impressed with me. I knew him well enough to know he wouldn't sulk for long, so I kept going despite him not saying another word.

"We needed to know what Bronson had planned next and I knew he would have a getaway bag somewhere in the house. It took me a while to find it, but it was worth it, wasn't it?" I grinned uneasily.

Tommo reached forward and picked up two of the passports, opened them up and raised his eyebrows as he flicked through the pages.

"These are very good quality. He must have a good contact to be able to get fake IDs this good," he remarked. I knew he was starting to be a bit impressed with what I had found, but he wouldn't let me know that yet.

Taking the passports off Tommo, Keira shook her head as she read off the fake details and names. "I really didn't know any of this, I promise." she moaned, clearly still processing how naïve she had been whilst she was under Bronson's spell.

"We know," I smiled, reaching out to squeeze her hand.

Tommo had now picked up the gun and was checking the chamber and the clip. "There's one in the chamber and the clip is full," he informed us. "This guy was well prepared to run.

"Well, he can't run far for now," I grinned, feeling a little smug.

"No, he can't, but this will only have delayed him for a few days, until he discovers this stuff is missing and has to source some new ones. Plus, he is going to know that someone has been in the house," Tommo grunted. He was clearly still furious, but at least he was now talking.

Tommo was right. It was clear that Bronson had contacts that could set him up with passports and fake IDs, and with the car business, he had the funds to set himself up again.

"There's something else in this bag." Nika announced as she fished her hand into the bottom of the bag and pulled out a tattered photo.

"What is that?" I asked, taking the photo from her to get a better look. It was photo of two small children, stood with what looked like their parents behind them.

The photo had a date on the back, written in faded blue ink: *Summer at the lake house '99.*

"Do you recognise this photo? I take it this is a young Bronson with his family," I asked Keira, holding it out to show her. But she shook her head and looked puzzled.

"I never met any of his family. He told me they all died in a car accident when he was young and he was the only survivor," Keira explained, shrugging her shoulders. "That was how we ended up dating: I fell for his sob story. I thought I had found a kindred spirit who understood the sort of loss I had been through."

"Did you ever meet any of his relations or did he ever tell you his back story?" I asked. I didn't want to bombard her with difficult questions, but there was something eating away at the back of my mind, that Bronson was not all he seemed.

"Nope, no one! No crazy aunts or distant cousins even," Keira replied simply.

"What's on your mind, Velvet? I can see something is making those clogs in your head turn." Tommo questioned, narrowing his eyes as if trying to see inside my head. He knew me far too well by now.

Ignoring Tommo for now, I shifted my weight on the wooden chair and turned my attention back to Keira. "So, no one from his side of the family came to your wedding? Just both your friends and acquaintances?"

Keira nodded, darting her eyes from mine to Nika's, then Tommo's, and then back again. "We had a very simple beach wedding with just a few friends. I don't get why that is so important." She sighed, clearly getting a bit tired of my questions.

"Look, I know this is difficult for you, but you will see why I am asking in a minute, I promise. Did you ever see any school photos of him or photos of him growing up?" I pressed. I was about to get the answer I needed; I was sure.

"No, nothing. Bronson told me they had all been lost while he was in foster care. Can you please tell me what the hell you are getting at, Velvet?" Keira snapped, flicking her long hair over her shoulder and folding her arms across her chest.

"Fine. Look this is just a crazy idea but, looking at the quality of the faked passports, I am wondering if Bronson Prince, is in fact Bronson Prince, at all. What if that is a fake identity too? What if one of these is his real name?" I replied quickly, tapping the passports with my finger.

"Jesus Christ, I never even thought of that," Tommo half laughed, clearly impressed. "Velvet, for a blondie you really do have a cracking brain."

"I'm not sure whether to take that as a compliment or not, Tommo, but thanks, I think." I grinned, giving him a wink.

The idea of Bronson not being Bronson, so to speak, had been flipping about in my mind for a little while, ever since I had found the passports and gun. He obviously had some decent contacts in the forgery game, and I had a strong feeling one of these passports was actually his true identity.

Keira was silent, her right hand clasped over her mouth as she tried to process what I had just said. I could just imagine what was going on inside her head, I would have to wait a few minutes before I asked any more questions. Nika, who looked equally as perplexed, stood up and took herself off to the kitchen, returning a few moments later with a half-bottle of brandy.

After giving us all a small glass, Nika sat back down in her seat and drank hers straight back. "So, this Bronson guy could be a totally different person. That's what you are saying?" she mused.

"That is what I am thinking, yes, but I could be totally wrong, of course." I shrugged, grabbing another slice of pizza and taking a large bite. "I really struggled to find anything out about Bronson online, and apart from his social media page and the 'Princeton Motors' website, there is nothing else. No school records, no newspaper articles, nothing. What if the paperwork Keira found was a clue to his real identity and that's why he's freaked out so much?"

"It does make a lot of sense, I will give you that," Tommo nodded, also helping himself to more pizza. "These sorts of things do happen, especially if people are trying to run away from something or someone. We now just need to do a little more digging with the names in these passports, see if we can work out where that photo was taken."

Keira was now drinking down her own brandy and was reaching to pour herself another, so I decided, before she got too drunk, I'd best ask a few more questions.

"Keira, I know this is hard and you have been through a lot, but we need to know as much as possible, okay?"

Keira drowned her second glass and nodded quickly. "Look, I know you need answers, but he honestly kept me in the dark about most of his business dealings. I was like a possession to him, like a car, I suppose. Something he could take out when he needed someone on his arm for a business dinner or social. I was always told not to ask too many questions when we did go out. Thinking back now I was just a part of his story, something to make him look legit to everyone else."

"Did you happen to spot any names on the paperwork you found that time?" I asked gently. "Any little clue as to who he could really be?"

"No. Like I said, I had literally just opened them up when he burst in and caught me. I really don't remember anything else. I'm really sorry." She answered glumly.

"It's okay, really," I nodded reassuringly, rubbing her shoulder. "You might remember more later on and if you do, just be sure to let me know."

"I promise I will." She smiled, looking a bit happier now.

"Grand Lake, Colorado," Nika pipes up suddenly.

"Sorry?" I ask, a bit confused.

"Grand Lake, Colorado. This is where the photo was taken." Nika replies, wafting the photo of the family in the air.

"You recognise it? Have you been there?" I beam, impressed that Nika has recognised the place from an old photo.

"No, it says so on the sign behind the family!" She laughs, sliding the photo across the table and pointing a perfectly manicured finger to the tiny sign in the background of the photo.

"Alright, clever clogs, I will admit I didn't take that close a look at it." I smile, sticking my tongue out at her.

Sadly, knowing where the photo was taken didn't give us any more clues as to who the people in the photo are or were. Are they really Bronson's deceased family or was that just a story he made up to hook up with Keira? Whoever they were, they were obviously important enough for Bronson to keep that photo closely hidden away from everyone and everything.

"So, let's have a look at these other passports then," Tommo suggests and slides a passport each to Nika and I to look at. Keira is biting her nails nervously as I flick through the passport I had, and we both take a sharp intake of breath when we see the passport photo. The person in the photo is quite clearly Bronson but his hair is bright blonde, just like the two young boys in the photograph. The passport says it was issued in 2019 and the name reads as Samuel Grantham.

"Well, hello there, Maxwell Wright." Tommo sings out, as he reads details from the passport he is holding. "Is this the same guy?" he asks, turning the passport round so we can all take a look.

"Yep, that's him. Well, a version of him or however you want to put it," Keira tutted.

The photo in this passport is clearly the same guy again but this time the hair is slightly darker and there is a slight shadow of a beard.

"So, who do you have, Nika?" I ask, twisting in my seat ready for her to reveal who she has found in the passport she is holding.

"Say hello to 'Benedict Johnson'." She smiles, showing us all a photo of the same guy, but this time the hair is dark, and he is sporting a neatly trimmed moustache.

"Interesting." I nod, not sure what else to say. Whoever 'Bronson' really is, he is quite the chameleon. We were going to have to do a fair amount of digging before we figured this part of the story out.

Using my cell, I started to type in the name on the passport I was holding and the date of birth, just to see if anything popped up. Nika and Tommo followed suit and a quiet hush fell about the room while we all studied any images that came up.

I decided to search for the name 'Samuel Grantham' and the words 'Grand Lake, Colorado'. Within a second, a raft of new articles popped up regarding a boating accident which had resulted in the death of three members of the same family, the Grantham's. The article revealed how a family boat trip had ended in tragedy after the youngest member of the family, Samuel Grantham, aged five, fell overboard and both parents dived in to save him. Sadly, due to strong underwater currents, all three failed to resurface and their other son, Thomas, was left stranded in the boat. He was discovered freezing and in deep shock a few hours later, by another passing boat, he was only seven. The article went on to say that Thomas was then raised by his maternal grandparents, Mr and Mrs Stonewich who lived in Scottsdale, Arizona.

The likeness between the old family photo and the passport photo of Samuel Grantham was uncanny. Thomas Grantham must have been the older brother of Samuel Grantham, who died tragically alongside his parents in in the lake. This could only mean one thing: Bronson was Thomas Grantham. But why had he changed his name to his brother's? We needed to do a bit more digging to find that out.

A few strong coffees later and after some serious internet research, Nika came across something else and spinning her laptop round to show the rest of us the screen, she explained what she had discovered. "Right so I was looking into the grandparents, the Stonewich's, from Scottsdale, Arizona. This is another newspaper article dated 5th January 2006 about a devastating fire that broke out at a farmhouse belonging to Edward and Rita Stonewich. The fire broke out in the middle of the night causing the farmhouse, and everything inside to burn to the ground. The remains of Edward and Rita Stonewich were found a couple of days later amongst the rubble and ashes."

"What about their grandson? Does it mention anything about Thomas Grantham?" I asked quickly, impatient to know the rest of the story.

"Apparently the body of fifteen-year-old Thomas Grantham was never found and his disappearance still remains a mystery to this day," Nika continued, raising her eyebrows at me. "Due to the sheer devastation left behind after the fire, police could not determine whether the fire was an accident or an act of arson. The case remains open."

We all took a moment to look at each other, wondering who was going to be the first to state the obvious. Bronson Prince must be Thomas Grantham, but why had he fled Arizona? Had he started the fire that killed his grandparents? This story was getting darker by the minute.

"I also found another article," Nika sighed as she tapped at the computer and brought another article up. "It appears the Stonewich's were pretty well off at the time of their deaths. This article is from a farming magazine a couple of years before the fire, which interviewed the Stonewich's about their cattle farm, and how they bred top quality, prize-winning bulls. There is a statement in this article saying that Edward Stonewich ran a tight ship and didn't trust the banks with his money."

"So, what happened to all their money? Did they keep it under their bed and go up in flames with the farm?" Tommo queried, rubbing his tiring eyes.

"Where do you keep yours?" I asked, with a playful wink, knowing full well that Tommo's ill-gotten gains were nowhere near a bank.

"So let me get this straight in my head," Kiera piped up. "You all think my husband, Bronson, aka Thomas Grantham, killed his grandparents and fled with all their cash to start a new life or lives?"

"I think that pretty much sums it up, yep," I nodded, pulling a face.

"But why?" Keira shrugged. "And why risk using your dead brother's name on a fake passport?"

"I can only assume that Thomas or Bronson didn't get along with his grandparents and wanted out. Whether he planned to kill them in the fire is another matter, and one for the cops to eventually figure out," I replied. "Using his brother's name was possibly a way of honouring him?"

This whole story was beginning to unravel like some sort of movie plot, and I was starting to wonder what else we would uncover. Had the trauma of watching his parents and younger brother disappear, beneath the dark waters of Grand Lake, kicked off some sort of crazy behaviour? It was possible, I suppose. If Bronson was Thomas Grantham, then he was more than likely still wanted by the cops investigating the death of his grandparents. If Thomas was innocent, he wouldn't have disappeared without trace and if the fire had been a tragic accident, his body would have been found in the burnt-out farmhouse, along with Edward and Rita's.

"It sounds like this guy has been quite twisted from an early age," Nika nodded. "I wonder how much more of this story is yet to be uncovered? What else has he done to get where he is now?"

"I don't know and I'm not sure if I want to dig any further to be honest," Keira shrugged, shaking her head slowly, whilst she fixed her eyes on the table.

"You don't need to be any part of this any longer Keira," I smiled softly, reaching for her hand again. "If Bronson is really Thomas, then the man you married didn't really exist at all. Sadly, your marriage was as fake as the rest of his life, and we just need to count our blessings that you survived it."

"So, what do we do now then, ladies?" Tommo asked gruffly. "It sounds like we need to have a serious chat with this Bronson, Thomas, whatever his bloody name is, before he either vanishes again, or his past catches him up. We could just tip off the cops and let them pick him up? They have more powers than us to prove who he is, and we can just sit back and watch him go down?"

"Get the cops involved now? Are you mad?" Nika growled. "This piece of crap nearly killed my friend, beat the hell out of Velvet and then tried to push Keira off a cliff in her car to cover up his dark dealings and fake life. He needs to be made accountable for his actions with something more than just a cosy prison cell. Can you imagine us explaining all this to the L.A.P.D. as well?"

Nika was right. If we tipped off the cops, we would need to have more solid evidence for them to act with any speed, and at the moment all we had was a photograph, some newspaper articles and an assumption. Without a DNA test to prove who he really was, we had nothing. The cops would probably think it was a fantasy, plus they would want to know why and how we had discovered it all. I certainly wasn't keen on telling them that I was out honey trapping when this all began. We would have to go after Bronson ourselves, and that wasn't going to be easy.

Chapter Twenty-Two

For the time being, I had decided to temporarily shut down the 'Black Blooms' website, so I could concentrate fully on dealing with Bronson. We all found it easier to call him Bronson, as this is what we had known him as. If he really was Thomas Grantham, we would deal with that later.

Our plan now was to somehow get Bronson on his own and expose him for whom he really was. I really wanted to see the look on his face when we told him about his failed attempt to kill Keira, and how we knew about him being Thomas Grantham. I wanted him to feel as vulnerable and weak as I did when he had his hands around my throat. The question now was: how do we get him on his own? It was apparent this guy was sharp, always on alert for anything suspicious and even with his fake passports and money in our hands, he would probably still be able to vanish at a moment's notice if needed. It was clear he had done this many times before, and I wondered how many lives he had torn apart before ending up in L.A.

'Princeton Motors' seemed to be the best place to confront him, but there was the danger of the Hulong people hanging around, and the last thing we needed was to be caught up in that mess. I figured it wouldn't be long before the Hulong people realised that Bronson had been filtering off some of their drug money to his own offshore account, that's if they didn't know already. We needed to be super careful and have a fail-safe plan. There was no room for any slip ups.

"So, who's going to the hardware store to buy the rope and duct tape? Those store workers will think we are buying a murder kit," Tommo joked as he arrived at my store the following evening, just as we were shutting up.

"Well, I guess that'll be me then," I pouted, rolling my eyes dramatically. "Don't worry, I will go to two separate stores to get the stuff, so I don't arouse suspicion."

Our plan was for Tommo to turn up at 'Princeton Motors' just before it closed for the day and pose as a potential buyer. Nika and I would be nearby and once Tommo convinced Bronson he was serious about buying a car, it was likely they would migrate to the office to seal the deal. Tommo then insisted that he would handle Bronson until we arrived, when we would help tie him to a chair. I took it that when Tommo said he would handle Bronson, he meant he would be armed. There was a darker side to Tommo that I knew existed and, being in the sort of business he was in, I suppose you had to know how to handle a gun well enough to protect yourself. It was a lot to ask him to do all this and he could quite easily have said 'No', and walked away. The reason he hadn't was because he knew Nika, and I, would go it alone if he didn't, so he wanted to try and keep us safe.

***

Two days later Nika and I were sat waiting a short distance from 'Princeton Motors', watching as Tommo pulled up in the car park in a clapped-out saloon he had borrowed from a friend. He had arrived just before closing and from where we sat, we could see both Bronson and another employee bringing in swinging advertising signs, as they prepared to close for the night.

"He looks so normal," Nika scoffed. "Look at him. Who would know that a few days ago he had left his wife to die?"

"I know what you mean. How can any human be so cold and brutal? How desperate do you have to be to have to wipe someone off the face of the earth, just to keep your dirty little secrets from surfacing?" I replied, shaking my head.

"I hope I never have to find out," Nika sighed.

Tommo had dressed in a plain light blue shirt tucked into a pair of dark denim jeans. For a drug dealer he didn't scrub up too badly and, noticing he slicked his usual wayward hair back it, was clear he liked to play dress up as much as me.

After ten minutes of watching Tommo, wandering about the cars with the young employee plodding behind him, pointing and gesticulating to various features, we became aware that Bronson had disappeared from sight. Taking out my cell, I sent Tommo a swift message telling him to ditch the salesman and find Bronson. Watching him type a hasty message, I waited for his reply which simply said 'I'M TRYING!!'

This was ridiculous, I felt like a caged tiger watching from afar and unable to get involved or at least help. I have never been one to have much patience and as I drummed my fingernails on the steering wheel, a plan was forming in my mind.

"What are you planning?" Nika asked me bluntly, folding her arms across her chest and giving me a knowing glare.

"Nothing. Well, not nothing, but we can't just sit here and wait, can we?" I tutted, ruffling my hair.

"Erm, yes we can just do nothing, as that is part of the plan we organised with Tommo. We just need to be patient and wait for his message," Nika snapped sarcastically.

Thinking of something to say in reply, I suddenly spotted Tommo talking to Bronson, and then the two of them headed inside the building, followed by the young salesman.

"We have lift off," Nika grinned. "See, I told you to wait and see."

We had to wait another twenty minutes before we watched the young salesman leave via the glass front door and cross the car lot to his own small red soft-top. A slight twinge of relief rose up inside me, but deep in my stomach, an ominous feeling was growing.

"I don't like this," I told Nika bluntly.

"For God's sake, Velvet, have you got no patience girl?" Nika groaned. "Tommo has gone inside with Bronson, just like we planned; the other staff member has left, just like we planned. Everything so far has gone to plan."

"I'm telling you now Nika, I don't like the feeling I am getting from this," I told her firmly. Tommo should have texted by now. Something has gone wrong." Before Nika could roll her eyes again and reply, I started the engine and drove towards 'Princeton Motors'.

"What the hell are you doing? Pull this car over now." Nika roared at me, but I wasn't listening. My gut was telling me something was off, and my mother always said 'Follow your gut', so I did.

Pulling into the parking lot as the sun was setting and casting long shadows across the parking bays, we both watched as the lights inside the glass-fronted building turned off one by one.

"Okay, I don't like this now," Nika exhaled, her eyes widening. "Why the hell are the lights being turned off?"

"I don't know, but we need to find Tommo, fast," I answered, pulling the car sharply up outside the now dark building.

"I'm going in. You get in the driver's seat and keep the engine running." I told Nika, leaping out of the car and slamming the door before she could argue.

The door into the main reception was still unlocked and as I pulled it open, I was met with almost complete silence. The faint hum of a computer was the only noise I could hear as I strained my ears. Where the

hell were Tommo and Bronson? Tiptoeing across the polished floor, the only sound now was my heeled footsteps echoing off the white-washed walls.
At the end of the corridor was an illuminated doorway, but still no sound. With my heart pounding, I made my way to the door, and knelt down to peer through the keyhole. I had to throw a hand to my mouth to muffle the sound of a scream that was about to make its way out from what I saw: Tommo was laid flat out on the carpeted floor, not moving at all, a trickle of blood was dripping from his mouth and his eyes were shut.

Falling back onto my backside, I clambered to my feet, only to feel my head being snapped backward, as someone yanked at my hair. Catching a brief glimpse of Bronson's face in the semi darkness, I fell backwards onto the hard floor. A sickening feeling of history repeating itself flashed through my head and somehow, I managed to twist my body away from the incoming blows Bronson was now trying to rain down upon me. Kicking my legs up I caught him in the groin, hard, causing him to buckle and release the tight grip on my hair. It was now or never. Jumping to my feet, I turned around and kicked him straight in the chin sending him tumbling backwards. Lunging for the door handle, I wrenched the door open and slammed it behind me. Dragging a heavy filing cabinet to wedge under the handle, I ran to Tommo, who was still motionless on the floor.

A deep pounding on the door told me that Bronson was now trying to ram his way in and apart from a small window, there was no way out of the office. We were trapped.

Shaking Tommo, I tried to rouse him, but it was clear from the injury to the back of his head, he was in no fit state to help me. Standing up I quickly surveyed the office, looking for anything I could use as a weapon, but there wasn't much apart from a desk and a chair. Yanking open the desk drawers I rummaged through, but the only sort of weapon I found was a silver letter opener. It would have to do.

With a crash Bronson burst into the office and we stood staring at each other, his face white with rage, breathing heavily.

"So what are you going to do now?" Bronson growled. "I'm betting you can't get through that window by the time I've reached you, but you best try because it's your only option."

"We know who you are, Thomas, so you best let us go," I replied. I had the letter opener in a fist-like grip behind my back, and I was now prepared to do whatever it took to get myself and Tommo to safety.

"So, you found out my real name. Congratulations! I also found out yours, Velvet Darke," He sneered, taking a step closer. You see, you are not the only person who uses the dark web to conduct their business and when your wife, sorry I mean ex-wife is as stupid as mine leaving her cell around for me to find… Well, it's amazing what you can find with a few clicks on a web page. When you have contacts like I have and one of them is an ex-cop, it is easy to find out who the small black car belonged to that kept driving past my house. Funny though you didn't look like a Mr Lin, more like the sweet little florist who lived next door to him and who borrows his car."

Beads of ice-cold sweat were running down my back, but I knew I had to keep my composure. "So, did you kill your grandparents? Was it you that lit the fire at their farm?" I fired back.

"My, you have done your research." Bronson laughed, "Do you really think I am going to tell you anything about me?"

"I know enough thanks," I replied, trying to keep my voice from shaking as I backed towards the window. "I also know where Keira is."

"So do I, but she isn't going to help you, is she? Not from where she is now, unless of course you are going to hold a séance," he taunted.

"No, you're right. Keira can't help me, but *she* can." I nodded towards the doorway.
Hearing a noise behind him Bronson span round, only to be hit square in the face with a fire extinguisher wielded by Nika.

Slumping into an unconscious heap on the floor, Bronson was spark out, blood trickling from both nostrils.

"That is for my sister," Nika yelled at his unconscious body.

"Your sister?" I gasped, my head spinning, but little pieces of this whole Nika and Bronson puzzle started to fit together. "I thought your twin sister lived in Florida?"

"She does. That's where she went after that animal attacked her. This is why I wanted him to pay so badly."

Nika spat, giving a still blacked-out Bronson a quick kick in his ribs.

"Why didn't you tell me it was your sister he attacked?" I asked, puzzled.

"Because I thought you wouldn't let me help you, if you knew I had a real personal link to him. I wondered if you'd think it might cloud my judgement, I guess," Nika shrugged, her anger now turning into emotion.

"Well, I know now, and we have to finish what we started, okay?" I nodded. I needed Nika back on track for this next part of the plan.

Nika nodded back her confirmation.

Scrambling to pull a cable from the back of a printer, we bound Bronson's hands tightly and then rushed to Tommo, who was now letting out some moaning sounds.

"I told you I had a bad feeling," I breathed, trying to get my shaking body back under control.

"I also experienced that same feeling when you disappeared inside the building, so I thought I best come to your rescue your ass, again." Nika winked. "What the hell do we do now?"

"We get them both into Tommo's car and you drive mine back to my apartment," I instructed, heaving Tommo into a sitting position, and tapping his face gently to wake him up.

"Velvet, he knew what we were up to," Tommo groaned, reaching for his head and wincing.

"I know, but don't worry about that now because we need to get out of here. Can you stand?" I asked gently, gesturing to Nika to help me lift him to his feet.

With Tommo safely in the front seat of the car, we ran back to get Bronson who was also now stirring from his unconscious state.

"We can't put him on the back seat, Velvet. What if he gets his hands free and tries to strangle you again?" Nika hissed.

"He isn't going in the back seat; he is going in the trunk," I grinned.

What I hadn't told Nika or Tommo, was that I had bought along the gun I had found at Bronson's house.

Throwing a glass of water at Bronson's face was enough to wake him fully and as he gasped and opened his eyes, he was met with the barrel of the gun, his own gun. I suddenly felt a wash of empowerment and control, although I was desperately trying not to show how much my hands were shaking.

"Get up," I told him. Grabbing him by the collar of his jacket and hauling him to his feet.

"You really think you are going to get away with this? You must know who I work for?" Bronson sneered, his eyes bulging in anger as I marched him towards the car park.

"Oh, don't worry, I know exactly who you work for and I also know you've been ripping them off and syphoning their money into a sneaky little account of your own. I really don't think they're going to be concerned with us, do you?" I replied, pressing the gun tight into his back until he flinched.

"If that's true, then trust me, you are as dead as me," He snorted.

"We'll see about that," I sneered.

It was almost dark outside now and although he hesitated slightly at the sight of the open trunk, Bronson obeyed my command to get in. Sticking a piece of strong tape across his mouth and slamming the trunk lid shut, I scanned the car park for any potential witnesses. No one was about and if they were, we would soon be well on our way. It seemed these days, a lot of things that went on were mainly unnoticed by the general public, who seemed too busy staring at screens to notice what was happening around them.

With Tommo in the front seat, still looking rather pale and Nika following in my car, we headed back towards my place. I still didn't know what we were going to do with Bronson once we got there and for now, I was more than happy for him to stay in the trunk.

"How are you feeling?" I asked Tommo tentatively, knowing that ultimately, I had put him in the situation that led to him taking a beating.

"My head and ribs hurt like hell, but I guess I will survive," He muttered, throwing me a sideward glance.

"I'm so sorry I dragged you in to all this." I breathed, reaching for his hand and squeezing it.
"What are friends for?" Tommo winced.

Pulling up at the rear of the row of stores, Tommo and I waited for Nika to arrive.

"Why are we back at yours?" Tommo questioned. "Surely you don't want him knowing where you live?"

"He already knows where I live and quite a lot of other things about me," I sighed. "It seems our friend Bronson has a dodgy ex-cop on his side."

"Great!" Tommo hissed. "That's just what we need now, an ex-cop henchman, who is probably watching us right now."

"You don't need to worry about him," I muttered under my breath.

"Velvet what do you mean; I don't need to worry about him?" Tommo whined. "What the hell have you not told me now, for heaven's sake?"

Allowing a little smile to spread across my face, I watched as Nika pulled into the parking bay. "Like I said, Tommo, you don't need to worry about this ex-cop friend of his. I will explain all in a minute."

Tommo just shook his head and muttered a few swear words as he followed behind me towards the back entrance to my store. Out of earshot from Bronson, but still keeping my eye on Tommo's 'borrowed' car in case he made an escape attempt, I started to explain to both Tommo and Nika what the next stage of my plan was. I knew they weren't going to like it, but I had to do this last piece of the plan by myself.

"So, a couple of days ago I was doing some digging on the SUV and its driver who picked up Bronson, the night he tried to kill Keira at 'The Overlook'. With a little help from Petra and her hacking skills, we managed to discover that the car belonged to a hire company based just outside the city. Using her magic powers to full capacity, we managed to pull up the driver's license of the guy who hired it. His name is Marcus Trevain, and after a little more digging, we found out that he is indeed an ex-cop, he ended up being an ex-cop after his name was tarnished by a fraud case he was mixed up in. It seems that both he and Bronson are mixed up quite tightly with the Hulong family, and I would imagine that he is also taking his own cut of the Hulong drug money. I contacted the Hulong family anonymously via another burner phone, and as you can imagine they were pretty mad to find out that Bronson was ripping them off. I sent them photos of the 'shampoo' bottles and his offshore bank account. Between us we agreed I wouldn't go to the cops about their rather large drug enterprise if they agreed to do nothing for one week and meet me tonight. As a little deal sealer, I told them about Marcus Trevain and I reckon they have already dealt with him."

Tommo just stared at me, and Nika put her hands on her hips and walked in a slow circle. I had really shocked them this time as I had gone back on my word of not going rogue again.

Taking one of the wooden chairs from inside the florist's, Tommo sat himself down and looked towards the ceiling as if he was trying to find the right reply written there. "Velvet, you do understand, you have well and truly kicked a hornet's nest doing all that? Especially talking to the Hulong family about Bronson. You do know they will just kill him and probably us because we know so much?"

"They have no clue who we are, like I said I used a different burner phone to contact them which I have now destroyed. How will they know who we are?" I replied shortly.

"Because when your crazy little plan of handing Bronson over to them takes place, you don't think they won't torture him until he tells them who you are? He knows where you work and live for Christ's sake!" Tommo growled, now looking me straight in the eye. They are dealing in millions of pounds worth of illegal drugs, and you have just blown the bottom out of their operation."

"You don't think I haven't already thought about that Tommo? I have done my research and I know how dangerous the Hulong family are, but you are just going to have to really trust me on this next part," I replied firmly. I knew Tommo wouldn't allow me to do the next stage of the plan alone and neither would Nika. I also had a back-up plan for that.

"So, what happens now?" Nika asked quietly. I could see she was looking seriously worried now and it made me feel slightly sick.

"I need to show you guys a video clip on my laptop; then I will explain what is going to happen next. Let's go and watch it quickly, then all will become clear," I smiled reassuringly. I could tell, neither were reassured.

Tommo didn't reply. He simply got up from the chair and shrugged his shoulders as I held open the door to the stairs that led up to the apartment.

"What about Bronson?" Nika asked hesitating slightly, as she remembered he was still locked in the trunk of the car.

"It will only take a minute, I promise, then we will get this all sorted," I nodded, gesturing for her to follow Tommo up the stairs. Watching as both of them got halfway up the stairs I shouted to them "I'm sorry, but I want you to stay safe," before I slammed the door shut on them and turned the key in the lock.

"Velvet, what the hell are you doing?" I could hear Tommo yelling as I headed back out of the store towards his car. I didn't reply and I didn't look back.

Chapter Twenty-Three

Screaming out of the car park, I drove out of the district and onto the main highway, my head pounding and my thoughts swirling in my head. I could hear Bronson kicking at the lid of the trunk, so I hit the brakes hard, slamming his body into the back seats. Hopefully that was warning enough for him to stop trying to escape. The meet up point was a thirty-minute drive across town, all the time I was praying the cops wouldn't pull me over and the heap of a car I was driving wouldn't break down.

I was heading for an abandoned and run-down motel just, off highway 405, and a mile before I reached the trackway leading down to it, I pulled over and stopped. Reaching for the small bag I picked up from inside the store, I rummaged inside and pulled out a short dark wig. Slipping it on and tucking all my hair into it, I made sure I was happy with its effect before carefully popping in some dark brown contact lenses. My hands were shaking by now so putting them in was less than easy, but I managed it. Blinking until they felt relatively comfortable, I next slipped on a pair of thin, black gloves and tied a dark scarf around the lower half of my face, tying it tightly at the back.

Approaching the motel, I took a sharp intake of breath as I saw the flashing lights of cop cars and swarms of armed officers patrolling the perimeter. Heading past the entrance I pulled over again, a short distance up the highway, and retrieved my burner phone.

"It's me. I'm driving a beat-up green Ford just off the highway and few yards up from the motel. He is in the trunk." I then ended the call.

A few minutes later, headlights filled my rear-view mirror and pulled in tight behind me. Stepping out of the car I headed to where a tall, dark haired, plain clothed cop was exiting his vehicle, his hand resting on the gun strapped to his waist. Popping open the trunk and standing to the side I waited while the cop walked up and looked inside. Smiling slightly, he grabbed Bronson under the arm and hauled him out of the trunk to his feet.

From the passenger side of the cop's car stepped a slim figure who wrapped their arms around their body to keep out the night's chill. It was Keira.

Bronson's face as he was reunited with the wife, he thought he had killed, was priceless and his knees nearly buckled beneath him. "Hi Bronson," Keira said quietly, sweeping strands of wayward hair from her delicate face. "You look like you have seen a ghost. It's such a shame all your little plans didn't quite work out how you wanted."

"So, Keira, you are confirming that this is your husband, Bronson Prince, the one that tried to kill you?" the cop asked calmly.

Keira nodded. "Oh yes, that's him alright."

"And can you tell me who this person is?" he asked, nodding his head in my direction.

"I've never seen her before in my life," Keira replied calmly, a brief look of gratitude and respect passing between us.

From his jacket pocket the cop revealed a thick, plain brown envelope and handed it to me. I nodded a thanks and, winking at Kiera, I headed to the trunk of the car and slammed it shut. Getting back into the driver's seat, I watched in the mirror as two other marked police cars pulled up alongside the plain-clothed cop and Keira, illuminating them in a pool of flashing lights. Moving out onto the highway, I joined the other traffic and put my foot down. It was time to go home.

I felt an overwhelming sense of peace as the flashing lights of the cop cars faded into the background, but it didn't last long. I now had to deal with Nika and Tommo who were probably still sat in my apartmentt, plotting their own ways of bumping me off. I had a lot of explaining to do and I needed to do some serious grovelling to win back their trust.

I really did need to rein myself in and try not to be so headstrong in the future. Tommo and Nika were part of my team, I needed to trust them enough to tell them everything I was doing, not just shut them out because I knew I might not always like their answer. I had always been a bit reckless. I couldn't help it. If I felt an urge to do something, it was usually overpowering enough to make me act before considering the consequences properly. I had been fortunate lately that my rookie actions hadn't killed anyone, and it was time now to take a more measured approach to how I dealt with things.

Tommo always had my back and even though I knew he would be mighty mad, I knew he would forgive me. Although, after tonight's efforts, locking him and Nika in my apartment, I guessed it might take a bit longer than usual.

Feeling for the package the cop had given me and tapping it with my fingers a small smile crept from the side of my lips. I was sure what it contained would be enough to stop any scolding from Tommo in its tracks, and it was sure to put a smile on Nika's face, too.

Finally pulling back into the parking lot behind the store, I hardly dared look to see if the back rear door had been kicked open, but it was still closed shut and everything seemed calm and quiet. Peeling off the wig and removing my contact lenses, I ruffled my hair, took a quick look at myself in the mirror, and steadied my breathing. It was time to face the music.

The door leading up to the apartment was still locked and as I twisted the key in the lock, I heard slow footsteps come a few steps down the stairs and then stop. Easing the door open, I was met with a stone-faced Tommo, who stood staring at me, his arms folded across his chest in his usual cross pose.

"Still alive then, I see?" Tommo snorted.

"Look, I can explain." I replied, sheepishly.

"You better explain real good," Tommo shrugged and turned to go back up the stairs. I felt like a teenager caught coming home late and having to explain to my parents where I had been and why I was late.

In the apartment Tommo slumped himself down onto my couch and Nika was stood gazing out of the window onto the street, looking just as angry as Tommo.

"I'm sorry, guys, I really am. I had no time to explain what was happening and I knew you wouldn't be keen to go along with what I had planned for Bronson," I sighed, peeling off my jacket and hanging it on the back of one of the dining chairs.

"Is he dead?" Nika asked bluntly, turning to face me, anger still flashing brightly in her amber eyes.

"No, quite the opposite. He is in Police custody, and I feel he is going to be there for quite some time." I half laughed, thinking about how control freak Bronson was now doing in a police cell.

"He has been arrested?" Tommo replied, sitting up straight on the sofa, his attention now caught by what I had said.

"It's a bit of a long story and I hope when you listen to what has gone on and why I did it, you might take it a bit easier on me?" I grinned through gritted teeth.

Walking over to the kitchen I reached for the top cupboard and took out a half-bottle of whiskey and three small glasses. Setting them out on the table, I gestured to Nika and Tommo to sit down and despite a couple of sighs and some eye rolling, they obliged.

"So, we know Bronson, Thomas, whoever he is, was dodgy, with more than a hint of dangerous. But, what we didn't look that closely into were the names in the other passports that I found at Bronson and Keira' s place. Do you remember one was in the name of Benedict Johnson?" I asked.

"The one with the moustache?" Nika replied.

"Yes, that's the one. Well, whilst Petra and I were looking up Bronson's cop friend, I also got her to look up the name 'Benedict Johnson'. Well, we were not disappointed in what we found. It turned out that 'Benedict' had a warrant out for his arrest for a failure to appear at trial for a serious fraud case. Now, we are talking millions of pounds of embezzled money, so pretty serious stuff. It was all to do with transfer of funds from a charity to a business buying medical supplies, except the money went missing on the way. It seems that 'Benedict' tried to say that the money was lost by the charity," I continued.

"So, he rips off charities too?" Tommo snorted., shaking his head. "He really is a charmer."

"Indeed he is, but it turned out that one of Benedict's, or Bronson's, or whoever he is, colleagues had been suspicious of him from the start. They'd kept photos and copies of everything he was involved in and with that proof, along with a tonne of other stuff, 'Benedict' was looking at a long time behind bars. He basically fled and went into hiding under another persona using the money to start up 'Princeton Motors'. Quite how he got involved with the Hulong family and got mixed up in the drug running and money laundering business, I don't know and, to be honest, I don't care," I explained.

"So how do the cops come into this and why should we still not be fearing for our lives?" Tommo asked bluntly.

"It's pretty simple, really. Like I said 'Benedict' had a warrant out for his arrest and also a pretty juicy bounty on his head, as it turned out." I smirked, watching a little sparkle begin in Nika's eyes.

"A bounty? Like from a bounty hunter?" Nika questioned.

"Well, kind of, except the money came from the cops when I handed him over to them tonight." I replied, pulling out the brown envelope the cop had given me and opening it. With a gentle shake I let the notes flow out on to the table and then sat back in my seat."

"Holy cow!" Nika beamed. "How much is there, Velvet?"

"$15,000, $5,000 for each of us." I grinned at them both. "It turned out that the cops were quite happy to pay up if I could hand over their man to them tonight. Don't worry, I went in full disguise so even the cops don't know who I really am. Not that they care now they have 'Benedict, Bronson, Thomas.' Whatever they want to call him."

"What about Keira? What happens to her now?" Nika asked suddenly, remembering that she effectively had a dead woman living in her apartment.

"Keira was there tonight when I handed over Bronson. She is making a full statement to the cops as we speak, about how her beloved husband tried to kill her at 'The Overlook'. Don't worry, she is keeping us all out of everything. She said it is her 'Thank you' for saving her life. I would imagine that when they find the car at the bottom of the ravine, that will be evidence enough for them to charge him with attempted murder as well," I answered.

"But what about the Hulong people?" Tommo grunted, starting to get agitated. "I cannot emphasise how dangerous these people are. They aren't just going to let us get away with destroying their cocaine business."

I knew Tommo would be freaking out about the repercussions of my actions, so I kept my voice low and calm. "But they don't know who we are, Tommo. If anything, I have done them a favour, tipping them off about Bronson and Marcus Trevain's betrayal, and I would imagine that 'Princeton Motors' will be stripped of anything illegal by now. Like you said to me before, these sorts of people are ready to up and move at the first sign of trouble so I would imagine that is what they have done. The cops turning up at our agreed meeting place tonight, with lights flashing and sirens blaring would be enough to have the Hulong family lying low for quite a while. There is nothing concrete to link Bronson with the Hulong family and their drugs operation. I would imagine Bronson is going to remain very tight lipped about any of that as he has enough charges piling up against him already."

With everyone delighted with the outcome of the Bronson saga, and satisfied of our future safety, we soaked in the moment in silence, smiling to ourselves. It was over.

Epilogue

Sorting the money into three piles, I slid a pile each to Tommo and Nika. "Nika, I know this is only a small amount compared to the revenge you wanted for what Bronson did to your sister, but I hope it helps in some way."

"Hey, look, I got to smash that piece of scum in the face with a fire extinguisher and throw him in the trunk of a car! That was priceless to me, and I can't wait to tell Amara that he finally got what was coming to him," Nika beamed, fanning her face with a wad of notes.

"So, are you like a Police snitch now?" Tommo grunted. I could see he was still not terribly happy with what had gone down tonight, but I could see he now looked a bit more relaxed after I had explained what happened.

"No, definitely not a snitch," I replied, shaking my head before knocking back my glass of whiskey. "More of a bad-ass bounty hunter for hire!"

"That job role sounds like a hell of a lot of fun to me," Nika winked, holding out her glass for me to clink in 'Cheers'.

"Well, to be honest, I might just go back to being a boring old florist for a little while until things properly settle down around here, but yes, I think this could be quite a nice little side-line for the future. Plus, the cop that handed over the money tonight was pretty damn hot, and I wouldn't mind bumping into him again," I purred.

"Velvet Darke, you will honestly be the death of me one day," Tommo moaned, resting his forehead on the table.

"But what a way to go!" I laughed loudly, wrapping my arms around his shoulders, hugging him tightly as he tried to fend me off.

"What about the 'Black Blooms' website? Are you going to shut that down or keep it going?" Nika asked, pouring herself another whiskey and topping up mine and Tommo's glasses.

"Oh, I will definitely be keeping that going for now and who knows how big I could grow a business like that? And, for the most part, it is a whole lot of fun and pays so well," I nodded.

"Well, you can count me in as a permanent member of the team if you like," Nika announced, holding her glass high. "I would like to make a toast to the three of us, a toast to our friendship and our future in the vengeance game."

"To us," I cheered, grabbing Tommo's arm, and raising it high. "And to tulips, peonies and blood tipped roses!"

The End.

Printed in Great Britain
by Amazon